PAULINE DEVINE was born in Loughrea, County Galway, and studied for a social science degree in University College Dublin. Later she attended Trinity College and Sydney University, where her subject was education.

She prefers ponies to processors and exhibits Connemara pony Sheeogue, a hardy and sociable soul, who likes winning rosettes and fancies being out in the field with the young horse.

Married, with one daughter, Pauline lives on the borders of Dublin and Kildare, where she looks after her two horses. She is treasurer of her local pony club and an exhibitor and prizewinner at the Kerrygold Dublin Horse Show. She also helps out with hunting and gymkhanas and enjoys going to schools to talk about – ponies and horses.

She has also written *Best Friends Again,* a sequel to this book; *Riders by the Grey Lake,* set in her native Galway; *The Hungry Horse* and *King Longbeard.* She was the first writer of children's books to be awarded an Arts Council Bursary.

Pauline Devine

BEST FRIENDS

Illustrated by Terry Myler

THE CHILDREN'S PRESS

To
John Michael and Lizzie

First published 1993 by
The Children's Press
an imprint of Anvil Books
45 Palmerston Road, Dublin 6

6 8 10 9 7 5

© Text Pauline Devine 1993
© Illustrations Terry Myler 1993

ISBN 0 947962 79 4

Typeset by Computertype Limited
Printed by Colour Books Limited

CONTENTS

1 BLUEBELL ARRIVES

It was a late spring evening and getting duskish. The sally-tree beside the house shivered at the promise of frost. I had been waiting all day.

The sound of an approaching diesel engine echoed up the hill. My labrador, Bono, dropped the ball. His loud barks shafted up through the air, muffling the screams of the opening gate.

I ran, yelling back to Dad that he'd arrived, that it was Grandad all right. We stood back on to the verge as his old jeep towing the green horse-box roared past, taking a stream of woodbine with it from the hedge. My leg wouldn't stop shaking. It always does that when I'm excited. My eyes fastened on the dark space above the ramp of the trailer for a glimpse of the pony inside. My dream pony!

'This way.' Dad waved him on.

The trailer scrunched and lurched and I yanked Bono out of the way as it rolled back on to the grass, to come to a sudden halt at a thumbs-up sign from Dad.

Grandad's big black hat barely fitted through the window. 'Am I all right there, Shane?' he shouted.

'Fine, Grandad. We can unload here.'

He slammed the cab door. 'Well, Sarah, you got what you wanted at long last. 'Amn't I a great oul Grandad to bring your pony the whole way up from Galway on me own?'

'Yes, Grandad, Thanks, Grandad.' Quick kiss and a hug for him, trying to see over his hat into the darkness of the trailer. 'Can we take her down now?' My leg was hopping like mad.

Grandad sprang into action. 'Hold on now till I get my stick.' Ducking down, his hand groped under the driver's seat and he shouted out to Dad, 'Okay, Shane, you can drop the ramp.' Then to me, 'Keep well back, Sarah.' Brandishing his cane, he circled us, darting in front and behind us, every side of us and stamping on the grass. 'Pull a bit of grass for her, Sarah. Have ye any thistles? She loves fresh thistles.'

Dropping on my hunkers I pulled a few wisps as Dad tried to undo some wires securing the ramp.

I held on to Bono's neckstrap and pulled at the tufts, eyes straying for a glimpse of tossing foaming mane, the thud of a proud hoof. But no, just Dad, with his tongue now hanging out as he worked away at more wire, string and nails.

'Need a bit of help there, Shane?'

'Got it!' said Dad, dropping the knotted binder-twine on the gravel. Then he eased down the ramp and stepped up on to it. Grandad called, 'Let her down easy. Don't fuss her. She'll walk down by herself if you take her easy.'

Before Dad's bulk filled the shadowed opening, I thought I saw a pair of ears, short and erect. Then he was back out again. He was smiling now. 'I'll take that from you Sarah.' Reaching, not for the new headcollar I held out to him, but the bit of grass.

Grandad nodded reassuringly at me. 'Wait until you see her. Just what you wanted.'

'Grandad, I couldn't sleep last night after you rang to say you'd be coming today. Did you see the new headcollar?' A small shuffling of straw bedding reached my ears and set my leg leaping madly again. Soft thud of a hoof on timber floor. Dad's voice in the distance. 'I'm taking her down now.'

'It's a dinky headcollar. Hold on to it. We'll be needing it in a minute. Now, stand back.' Grandad's stick waved again. 'Keep back that dog. Right, Shane. Reverse her out.

Take it easy though, that ramp is slippy.'

It was taking Dad a long time and I wondered if the pony was too strong and powerful for him. Ever since I was three years old, Grandad had been promising me a pony – a dark grey with a white blaze and three white socks. Any second now, I would pat her for the first time, speak to her in a quiet voice to calm her down and gently lead her about to help her get over her fear of her new, strange surroundings: later on, possibly ride her. Up until now, I hadn't ridden very much, only on my cousin's old pony when I went to Cork on holidays. This pony would be young, full of power, fit to carry me to victory on the school's riding team.

Our house is located on the north side of Tooten Hill, near the village of Griffeen in County Dublin. From where we're standing, there is a view of five counties – Dublin, Wicklow, Kildare, Louth, Meath – and on a clear day the mountains of Mourne can be seen for good measure under the big bowl of sky.

'Clear the way!' The pony's hind quarters appeared on the top of the ramp and slowly Dad reversed her down. Reaching the bottom, she stood beside him, looking out from the circle of his arm. My dream pony! My leg stopped dead and a long moment went by as I looked at her, speechless.

Then my eyes travelled past her. Down over the black roofs on the slope, the clump of village houses at the bottom and, beyond that, to the pale gloomy fields of the Liffey valley. The sun did not shine today as promised. No sudden flash of cheer or colour.

Slowly my eyes returned to the slope. Half way up, on the far side, they stopped to rest on the large windows of a dark house. Me and Babs Tipping had been best friends. That was before she had begun to tease. Cold air seeped through my sweater and I shivered.

I wanted the pony, so that I, Sarah Kleptoria Quinn,

could shine like a star among my friends. In school they would be begging me for an invitation to come to my house and see her, maybe even have a ride. And I would pick and choose one or two and say sorry to the others. Next time. Babs of course would be welcome every time; that is, when I wasn't visiting her place. And I would never again have to sit on the bench in the school playground because no one would play with me.

'Sarah! Easy now. Don't frighten her.' Grandad was beside me, talking cheerfully to me, telling me to come closer to my pony. 'There you are, Sarah, just what I promised, isn't it? A young grey mare with a white blaze, the three white socks. Isn't that what you wanted?'

'Yes, Grandad,' I answered and slowly, full of dread, I approached, careful not to touch the mangy coat. Not able to speak or look at him, just nodding, eyes scanning the ground, looking for a hole to hide in.

'Give her another little pick of grass. Easy now.'

'Yes, Grandad.' Obediently bending down to pull some more, I sneaked another look at her, at the strong ugly jaws working away, the undersized ears flickering on top of her white baldy face. As for her bristly coat, she looked like the hedgehog I once rescued from the pit of a cattle grid. Worst thing of all was her size, her shoulder barely up to my shoulder-blade.

A nettle brushed against my hand and stung me. All at once, a nasty feeling broke out all over me. What would Babs and my other friends say when they saw her? Not to mention my enemies. This was just great! Dream pony? More like a nightmare! Grandad had let me down badly.

We'd have to get rid of her. And quickly. I looked for Dad's eye but he was forking old bedding from the trailer.

Grandad was gripping the pony's mane. 'Don't mind giving her that old coarse grass. Pull her a sweet bit. Over here! Dandelions are great for her. Pissy beds we used to call them. Great for the kidneys!'

I pulled where he directed, near the septic tank, still trying to catch Dad's eye. But he just didn't realise. There he was, petting the shaggy mare.

I knew I should be very grateful to Grandad, for driving up the whole way from Galway with that pony. There was no way he could have afforded a really expensive one. I knew that. He had money enough only to pay for his own funeral, and no more. I heard him myself tell Uncle Sam that, when Sam asked for a loan.

But surely he could have managed to get me something better. Now we would have to ask him to take her away.

Grandad dropped down on his knees beside me and started pulling at the grass. 'Here, give her that now,' adjusting his hat back on.

She ate eagerly out of my hand. 'Well, Sarah,' Dad's voice was gentle in my ear, his hand rubbing the pony's neck. 'What do you think of her?'

'She's a grand pony, isn't she? A real live wire.' Grandad looked at me expectantly.

'Well, I . . .' I'm looking down at my jodhpurs, my cousin's cast-offs; by now I should have been sitting tall in the saddle, riding around the field on my pony. The rubber riding boots were beginning to pinch. I couldn't wait to throw them off. 'She's just a youngster. She has no experience,' Grandad said. 'You'll have to train her.'

'Grandad!' I couldn't keep quiet any longer. 'I'm not so sure I'll be able to handle her. How can I train a pony?'

He looked at me, mouth open in surprise, and I thought now is the time to tell him. I don't want her. I looked around for Dad for support but he was emptying the wheelbarrow in the rhubarb path. I felt something warm under my hand and realised it had somehow come to rest on the pony's neck.

Suddenly Grandad's arm shot out and he grabbed the pony by the bob. 'Put on that headcollar and lead her around. It's time you got used to her. Here, I'll do it.'

'No, Grandad, I'll do it. She's my pony.' That headcollar I'd bought, paid for with my own money. For my pony.

He let go. 'Stand in to her so.'

After trying it on her backwards and upside-down a few times, I managed to slip her nose into the headcollar, then buckled it behind her ear. I stood at her head holding the lead rope which Grandad had already attached to the head-collar, while he fussed about checking that it was properly fastened. 'Shorten it under the chin. That's right.' He nodded in satisfaction.

I pulled at the rope, then stopped. The little pony was looking strangely at me from under her crispy dry fringe. 'Grandad, what's wrong with her eye?' This pony was full of unpleasant surprises!

'Where? Show me.' In silence he peered at her through his glasses. 'Not a bit of harm in the wide world. It's what you call a wall-eye. A prod of a branch would cause that but she'll grow out of it.' He stroked her rough coat. 'Isn't she a grand colour?' slapping her enthusiastically. 'Walk her on now.'

But the pony was in no hurry. Neither was I, blinded for a moment by the white dust rising off her back that spread like a white mist around us before settling lightly on the grass. 'What's that stuff?'

'Only dandruff,' he answered. 'I've already checked her for lice. It's no harm to her at all. She'll thrive on this good grass and get rid of all those ailments.' He was looking around him. 'Now, have ye decided where to put her?'

Dad propped the fork against the trailer and came over. 'We've more or less settled on the paddock there.' He nodded in the direction of the small grassy field that ran along by the driveway between the house and the road. Dad and I had decided on it because, as well as being close to the house, it was well fenced, with some furze bushes along by the ditch. So sheltered from the wind that primroses were already peeping up there.

Grandad walked over and pushed against the fence to test its strength. 'Ideal, that will do the finest. Later in the year when it starts to get cold, you could put her in at night. You'd need a bit of a shed for her. Now, I've a grand lot of sheet iron at home that you could have.'

Dad laughed loudly. 'No thanks!' The pony's ears twiddled at the sound. Last year, Grandad brought us a lot of old iron railings and we had to cart them to a scrap-heap.

'All right so,' he muttered. 'But they were good railings, only the oul bit o' rust.' He moved off.

He was rooting in the cab, throwing old pieces of leather out on the ground. 'You'll be needing some riding equipment, Sarah. I have stuff here that will be useful to you. Look at this!' With some effort he lifted it up proudly. The saddle was dark and bulky, its lining torn, and it smelled strongly of must. The leathers and the rusting stirrups were mismatched. 'An antique,' passing it on to Dad. Pulling out more stuff. 'I found these in the stable at home,' holding up bits of leather, an old set of broken reins, an old bridle held together with baler twine, a broken noseband, mildewed and cracked. 'Do you remember oul Jack?' he asked Dad. 'Your uncle Paddy, er, my uncle Paddy had him for years. A great plough horse. Powerful. As good as any tractor. These tacklings were belonging to him. Thrown out for years they were and no one ever bothered to take them in or look after them. They'll be useful to you while you're training the pony. Just give them a rub of saddle-soap to soften them. Ah, the bit. That goes in the pony's mouth.' It was huge, made of copper, and had a dent in it that must have been caused by a giant's tooth.

'But, first things first. It'll be a while before you can put the saddle and bridle on her. For a start, you'll have to school her a bit.' He was fiddling with bits of reins.

'Grandad, I don't know anything about teaching ponies. I wouldn't have a clue!'

'Don't worry. We're going to give her a very first lesson

right now.' He told me to take off the headcollar. 'Shane, get me a hammer and nails!'

After straightening the big rusty nail and punching it through the headcollar, he said, 'Now, a ring. Any old brass or copper curtain ring will do.'

I found one in the boxes of scrap in the tool-shed. He attached it to the headcollar, drew the rope through it and knotted it. 'That ring pulls the pony forward. Put it on her, Shane.'

Dad fastened it. The pony looked even more miserable.

'Lead her on!' Grandad's voice rose impatiently.

A light tug on the rope this time and the little pony walked after me through the small gate into the paddock. She stopped when I stopped and looked over at me. Then something began to bubble up inside me, a warm feeling, different from before. I thought, 'This pony belongs to me.'

'We're going to lunge her,' Grandad said to me, striding into the middle of the field. 'Seeing as this is her first lesson, you'll need a lot of patience. We're going to take her around in a circle, to the right and to the left. You stand at the centre and get her to circle around you, and you should need only a light pull on the rope. Yes, like this. When you want to stop, say 'Whoaa!', draw her to you, pat her and lunge her in the other direction. In this way she learns when to go and when to stop, and to bend her body. By right you should have a lungeing whip. I went to get a loan of it from Mick Burke but he was after lending it to Dan Donnellan and never got it back. Always the same, you couldn't get anything out of him . . . Here, give me the rope and I'll show you.'

Snatching it from me, he shortened it and walked around in a circle with the pony, keeping close to her head. Then he moved to the centre, lengthening the rope, and showed me how to hold it before handing it back to me.

'Go on,' he said to the pony.

The pony took a few steps forward. After further louder

instructions from Grandad, she trotted a little and stopped, then looked back at him inquiringly, as if she was wondering why he wasn't walking with her as before. Dad was over by the fence watching.

'Drive her on!'

I shook the rope behind her and she took a few lazy steps sideways. Grandad moved into action. 'Go on.'

She was trotting about in a kind of a circle with Grandad running behind. Her head was up and she looked unhappy. When he stopped, she stopped and looked back at us. 'Go on again.' Grandad was breathing fast and his face was red. She trotted off in front of him once more. But her concentration was not on what she was doing and she kept turning to look back at him, one ear cocked in surprise.

Dad called to Grandad to take it easy. I, too, wished he would stop in case he got another heart attack. I tried clicking my tongue, hoping that would get her to move. But she was not interested. That is, until Grandad's hat fell off;

then she trotted over and looked at it with a kind of friendly
stare.

I stepped up. 'Keep away, Grandad,' I heard myself say.
'You're only distracting her. I'll do it on my own.'

He fingered the dent in his hat. 'Go on, so,' waving us
away in disgust. A determined feeling gripped me.

At first, when I shook the rope at her, she just trotted in
to me and nudged me. For some reason, my knee gave a
small hop.

'Don't let her do that! Keep her going!' Grandad, with
his hat back in place, was doing a bit of a dance by the
fence. 'If that's the way you're going to train her, you'll get
no rights of her at all,' he bawled. 'You'll destroy her. Spoil
her and she'll be good for nothing.'

Calmly I ignored him. Maybe there was a reason why she
was turning back all the time. Maybe she wants to go in the
opposite direction, anti-clockwise.

Easy girl, easy. Quietly I led her out again and walked her
around to the left this time, firstly on a short rope, gradually
lengthening it. No fuss, although Grandad was poised for
take-off, mouth open, hat in his hand at the ready.

She was trotting for me. 'Trot, trot, trot, trot,' Grandad
called out in time to each stride. 'Now she's getting used to
it. That's the way. A lot of ponies go better to the left. Trot,
trot, trot, trot – talk to her. Bring her back to a walk. now
get her to stop.'

My 'Whoaa' was one long calm sound and she stopped.
Then I got her to trot again, a brisk rhythmic trot. I caught
Dad's eye. He was smiling and nodding.

Her head was up. She was distracted again, looking
around her. Grandad said, 'It'll take her a while to get used
to it. Just be firm with her. Send her around again.'

Bono came to the gate, tail wagging, followed by light
footsteps. It was Mam.

'Well, what do you think of her?' Grandad's head was
jerking enthusiastically.

'She's a lovely little animal. And seems so quiet too.' Mam gave her a light pat, her voice sounding relieved as if she were glad it wasn't an Arab stallion or something. 'What age is she?' She looks as if she's only a baby.'

'Mam, she's not a baby! She's a youngster.'

'She's rising four or maybe five.' Grandad patted her hairy coat. 'See?' He caught her by the jaw and her mouth opened. We all peered inside. She smelled of old flowers in a vase. 'You know by the teeth.' They looked a fair grown size to me.

'Do you know why she has gaps each side, between her front and back teeth?'

'The teeth haven't grown there yet?'

'No. That gap is where the bit goes.'

'What's the bit for?'

'The bit is the part of the bridle that brings you in contact with your pony's mouth, so that you can stop or steer.' He let go and her mouth closed again. 'Get me that one I brought up.'

It was as big and heavy as the bone the butcher gave us for Bono. How was a little pony going to carry that in her mouth?

He scrutinised it. 'Now, this is probably too big for her. You might need to get a smaller size.'

'I think so, Grandad.'

It dropped with a clang and he said, 'She's at the right age for schoolin', even though she looks younger than her age because of the poor feedin' she got. Above on the side of a bare mountain where there was nothing but bog and rocks. But in a few months time, with the good grass and the bit of schoolin', you won't know that pony.'

'Schooling? Is there much involved in looking after her?' Mam casually picked a dog hair off her new black and white ski pants but a small frown had appeared on her face. Already she had told me that I would never look after a pony, that I would lose interest in riding in a short time and

the pony would be left to her to look after – only she was
not going to do it. I'd drop out; it would be like the speech
and drama and the swimming and the karate and the fenc-
ing, not to mention music practice.

'You won't have to worry about that, Mam.' A pony was
different and I was determined to show her.

'There will be no lookin' after at all,' Grandad answered.
'Sure, she'll be out on grass. She might need to be fed a few
nuts as well. But the main thing is the bit of schoolin'.

Dad interrupted. 'Speaking of feeding, isn't it time we
had our tea?'

'Let's go inside.'

'We'd better put the pony in first.' Grandad took her rope
from me.

'Grandad!' Running, I caught up with him at the paddock gate. There was one very important question I had to
ask. 'Grandad, when can I start riding my pony?'

'Any day soon,' he panted. 'Her back is a bit soft yet. But
the lungeing will make a job of her.'

'How often should we do it.' I pulled back the catch for
him.

He led her through. 'Do it every day, but only for short
whiles. Then you can sit up on her when your father is
lungeing her. For twenty minutes or so at a time. She's
quiet. I think we'll let her off now.'

Grandad wasn't ready for his tea just yet. He was saying,
'I'd like to get some nuts for that pony. She needs some
extra feedin' to bring her on a bit. Grass hasn't that much
nourishment in it yet.'

Dad's voice sounded weak. 'I think it's time we ate a bite
ourselves.' That meant he was starving. 'Don't worry about
the pony. I'll get her some nuts on my way home tomorrow.'

But Grandad was already striding towards the jeep. 'You
wouldn't know what to get, Shane. It's better to leave that

to me. They're a special type that Johnny Watchmacallhim told me about. Is there any good shop around that might have them?'

I told him about the shop in the village – the quicker my pony fattened up the better.

Grandad's nose was pressed to the windscreen as we flew down the hill, heads bouncing off the roof of the cab.

The shop was closed. 'The shop in Newbridge might be open,' I told him. 'But you'll have to drive down the dual carriageway.'

'Ah, sure, I drove on that "lean-to" before.'

'Grandad,' I grinned over at him. 'It's not a lean-to. It's a by-pass.'

Grandad started up again. 'A by-pass or a lean-to or whatever you call it. We'll be on it.' He added, 'If there's a medical hall open, remind me to get some worm powders for her too.'

He was a bit mesmerised driving out on to the dual carriageway with the lights and all. He gnawed at the steering-wheel waiting for the lights to change. 'Go, Grandad, go!'. But just as the lights turned green, the jeep stalled. Then, as they turned to red again, we shot off, leaving a queue of cars behind us.

'Is this the place?' He stopped the jeep right outside the door of the shop. 'We'd better park here in case there's any joyriders about.'

Grandad told the assistant the type of pony nuts he wanted and they went off together to the store. He came rushing through carrying a big sack. Just as well I was holding the glass door open for him. Outside on the street he collided with a man on his way to the pub next door. The man put down his long case to help Grandad. He flicked his beard out of the way and tossed the sack into the back of Grandad's jeep, dusted his hands on his jeans. The two of them shook hands and went into a huddle, heads together.

I waited. 'Sarah!' Grandad was calling me over. 'Meet a

very good friend of mine, Chris Beresford. Chris, this is my granddaughter, Sarah. I'm after buying her the grandest little mare you ever laid eyes on.'

'If she takes after her grandfather, she'll be a fine horse-woman.' The man with the beard smiled at me. His jeep, parked beside ours, had the figure of a horse on the bonnet.

'I thought you were in Kentucky,' Grandad was saying.

'Coming and going all the time, Dinny. I'm specialising now, you know.'

They were talking about Galway. Chris was asking Grandad something about a tune. 'A fine old reel,' he was saying. 'One I'd like to have.'

'Ah, sure, I often meant to record it and send it on to you. But I had no way of doing it.'

I interrupted. 'You could have taped it, Grandad, with that tape-recorder we gave you for Christmas.'

'Would you believe?' Grandad wrinkled up his lips in disgust. 'Granny never learned how to use it.'

'I'll record it on my Sony stereo system. We'll do it tonight.' Here was a brilliant reason for staying up late.

'She's a great girl. The best of my grandchildren.' Grandad beamed at me and I felt myself going red.

He was in a hurry now. 'I haven't time for that drink, Chris. The tea will be ready for us. And I want to check on the pony.'

I hopped into the cab. Chris shook Grandad's hand solemnly and said, 'Don't forget about that tape. Ancient music like that must be recorded for posterity.' He gave him a printed card. 'Post it to that address.'

'Is he a musician?' I asked as we drove off.

'No. A vet. A great man with horses.' Grandad chuckled. 'But he's stone mad on Irish music. He's lookin' for an oul tune he heard me hummin' one time. He plays the banjo. And he's not bad at that either.'

As we passed under a street lamp I read "Christopher Beresford, Simmonscourt Hospital, The Curragh.'

'It's a horse hospital,' Grandad explained. Then he groaned. 'We never thought of asking him for the worm powder.'

The pony's white face was sticking out through the bars of the fence watching us as we drove up to the house.

Little spurts of light were brightening up the evening sky as I leaned on the fence and took stock of my pony again. Okay, she was a bit small. But she'd grow, Grandad said. I narrowed my eyes, pretending I'm Babs, only that's not easy. She's so good-looking with her black bouncy hair and big shiny green eyes, while my shoulder-length hair stays thin and stringy no matter how often I wash it, and my eyes are a watery grey. And of course, on account of my ears, I can never wear my hair in a ponytail. Never! They're like pencils. The pony's mane and tail are too long and thin, but they can be cut and brushed and combed into shape. Her colour – grey with faint flecks of something else, maybe white, maybe silver. Babs and I will wash her with suds. She would like that. Piles of suds. But right now, I thought, the most important thing was to find a name for her.

She pecked away at the grass, with every bite drifting further away. Then she stopped eating and her head was up, as Bono came slinking towards her, tail wagging eagerly. She waited until their noses touched and they sniffed each other. Then her head went back. She took him by surprise but he just managed to duck away as she pounced at him. After that near miss, she swung about with a sharp movement and took off in a fast gallop up the centre of the paddock. She stopped, neck arched, legs spread apart, snorting loudly. Then she was off again, her hooves dancing over the turf, barely touching it as she sped along. Twisting and turning she drew near to Bono again and charged straight at the spot where he stood rooted to the ground, head cocked in amazement. At the last second, he took off and slid out under the gate to safety, ears close to his head, tail

sideways in rejection.

Slithering to a halt near beside me, sides heaving, nostrils flaring, she watched me steadily. A small movement from Bono and she whirled away again from the fence. She pranced about, tail up, lifting her hooves high, like a pony in the dark loaded with jewels. That warm feeling that was bubbling around inside me suddenly burst and flooded right through me.

I understood what she was up to. She was showing off. Showing off to Bono and me. And, I knew, just the same as if she could talk, that she was proud and happy to be here. She was home.

I waited outside until it got dark and she had moved up to the far end of the paddock, seemingly content, grazing away.

At supper I said, 'Grandad, I've thought of a name for her. I'm going to call her Bluebell.'

'Bluebell?' Grandad slowly picked up his spoon, put it down. 'What sort of a name is that? I don't like it at all. Can't you call her "Veni Vidi Vici" or "Spring Tide" or "Harvest Time" or something?' His head lifted again and he said hopefully, 'There was a great horse down my part of the country once called . . .'

'Grandad,' biting firmly into a sausage, 'I saw that programme on the Bluebell Girls, the Paris dancers, on the telly. My pony is a dancer. If you saw her just now, dancing on her tiny hooves you'd know there is no other name for her.'

'I dunno.' Grandad got up, and even though Dad was calling to him to have sense, to sit down and have his meal, he went to the window. The pony was racing about the field in the dark, hooves drumming.

'Bedad, she can go like the wind all right. But, is there no other name you could call her?'

'Grandad, her name is Bluebell. Bluebell Mountain.'

'Well, all right so.' With that he gave up and came back to the table.

'She likes it here.' I told him, sucking at a rind.

'And why wouldn't she.' Grandad pushed away his plate. 'That wan will turn out a beauty yet. You'll be winning competitions all over the country with her.'

'So long as she's quiet.' Mam placed a plate of lamb cutlets in front of him. I helped myself to some of Dad's coleslaw.

After supper I went out to the porch to investigate the bits of harness Grandad had brought with him. Wiping them clean with a damp sponge, I left them to dry, before rubbing in some vegetable oil to soften the leather and hanging them up at the back of the door.

As I came back in, Grandad was saying, 'If Sarah can earn the love and trust of that young pony, she'll have earned a very valuable thing that will stand to her for life. You see, long ago, there was always a bond between an owner and his horse. They were together all day, working side by side in the bog or abroad in the field. The owner got to know his horse well and the horse knew him, d'ye see. Sure, in them times a horse often carried a man home while he'd be sleeping in the back of the cart, after being all night in the pub. That same bond isn't there anymore.'

I gave Grandad my room where he would be cosiest. A chink of the guest-room door was open to let in light from the hallway and through it came Mam's voice from the kitchen. 'Everything is rosy in the garden now. But I wonder how long it will last.'

Then Dad's, 'I know she's been fickle about the other activities she took up. But I've a hunch it will be different with the pony. It's a living thing.'

'I hope so. but if that pony interferes with her homework she'll have to go!'

Something else great happened that night which I almost forgot to mention. It was about Mr. Tipping.

While I was standing at the door of the shop waiting for Grandad, Mr Tipping came out of the pub.

'Hi, Mr Tipping.'

He paused and came over. As soon as I told him I was Babs' friend, he knew me straight off. 'Babs' friend. You're Babs' friend.' Reaching into his pocket he took out a note – a £5, which he handed to me. After that I helped him get his key into the car door.

Probably had his briefcase stuffed with duty-free stuff for Babs.

Afterwards I remembered I hadn't told him about the pony. I was glad. I wanted to surprise Babs.

2 TRAINING

Our school is only a few minutes by bus from our house, around the hill and down the main street of Griffeen and it's on your right-hand side, beside the church. You could walk there only that the road is so narrow and there is no footpath. Once Babs took a header off her bicycle when it ran into a pot-hole.

'You're up early, Sarah. It's only eight o'clock, you know,' Smart of Dad to notice; it's usually ten minutes to nine before I appear. Today I'd already been out to see Bluebell. She had stood up and allowed me to pat her.

'Dad, can you give me a drive to school?' I wanted to tell Babs about Bluebell before class began.

'Yes, but hurry.'

I gobbled a few cornflakes, while Dad stood there rattling his car keys. Going out I shouted to Mam, 'Tell Grandad not to leave before three o'clock.'

He might like to meet Babs when she came to see my pony; Babs Tipping had been my best friend for a long time. She can be great fun, when she's not teasing, but since Katie Spillane's family came to live near her in the old mill house, her teasing has got worse.

We don't get a chance to talk much until break-time because Sir makes her sit in front where he can 'keep an eye on her.' Today I hoped she would be early. I waited at the gate but class had begun before she arrived.

'Sorry, Sir,' her jewellery jangling loudly as she hopped from one leg to the other. 'My Dad's plane was late getting in from Brussels last night and we were all up late 'cos we were looking at what he brought us from duty-free so we

25

slept it in this morning.' She grinned at us all. In her hand she was holding up a small box for Sir to see and ask her what it was, so that the whole class would notice.

Sir grunted. 'Sit down and take out your maths book.'

When he left the room to go to the Principal's office, Babs took out the little box again and she and Katie examined it. Perfume. Katie was smelling her wrists.

I did one long division sum. There was no way I could keep it to myself any longer. Beside me, Niall Hickey looked up from his copy-book, eyes widening under his hayloft of hair. 'You got a young pony? Hey, that's brilliant!' His voice dropped to a loud whisper as he added, keeping one eye on the door for teacher, 'Look, me and Trevor usually go out the road on our ponies after school. Do you want to come with us? Today, if you like. It'd be no problem.'

I felt myself getting red. 'Well, not really. Bluebell isn't ready to go on the road yet.' I was looking past him.

On Niall's far side, Trevor Boylan had been having a word with Susan, probably about the disco last night. They're both allowed to go. Trevor is Niall's best friend. He wins lots of prizes on his pony. At the mention of his name, he had stopped talking and was looking over at us. He flashed a fifty tooth smile. 'Riding is a bore,' he said. 'I prefer motorbikes.' He was so cool.

Babs was looking around, eyes stopping short of our desk. I quickly scribbled a note to her. 'Come down after school to see my new pony' and watched it being passed up through the desks to her.

Sir came back and she put it away, not looking around. Just gave a small smile. At break-time, she was out in the playground before me, racing around with Mona and Emma, shouting and laughing, looking over in my direction. I'm in the shelter where I usually sit when no one will play with me. I'm on my own. You have to have a note from your parents if you are not feeling well and want to

stay back in the classroom. Mam won't give me any more notes.

Babs has broken away from the others. She zoomed in my direction, semi-circled the bench, one, two, three times, grinning. She wants me to play after all.

'Babs, can I be on?'

She stared at me, then ran screaming out of the shelter, Emma and Mona flanking her each side, their laughter cracking off the school walls like a whip.

I should have known she'd be in one of her teasing moods. During the last few months she has been teasing more and more and I don't know what to do. After a row, I always have to make it up. They came back beside me, Babs silently mouthing, laughing and jumping up and down, calling to the others, saying something. I can't hear.

'Babs, will you be down after school to see my pony?' Dancing up and down, bandy legs lifting, black pigtail swinging, mouth slightly open showing her sharp teeth. 'I mightn't be able. I'll try,' she panted. She grinned across at

Katie who's joined them. They're asking her to play.

I got up. 'Babs, can I play too? Please.'

'Sorry,' eyes triumphant. 'We've too many already.' They circled me, hemming me in, and Babs' arms were like steel, forcing me down again. Then from somewhere in the distance a bell rang. Suddenly she yelled to Katie, Emma and Mona, and they ran away.

Still, I'm hoping she'll be down after school. It will be exciting training the pony with her around. I tell you, when she's in a good mood she can be so funny.

Bluebell watched me opening the gate, her small ears cocked at the roar of the bus, two front legs together and her back ones daintily spread apart. I ducked in under the fence and she nuzzled me warmly in welcome, putting a streak of green slime on my school jumper but it rubbed off easily on the sleeve of my coat.

Grandad's jeep was still there. He was in the kitchen with his hat on, plastic bag in his hand. Ready for the road. He pointed to a tangled heap of leather and ropes on the table that he had put together. 'You'll be using them when you're taking the pony out on the road and learning how to steer her. Next time I come you should be riding her. I've shown your father how to work the long reins.'

'I hope this pony isn't going to take up too much time,' Mam said. The frown was back.

'Not at all,' Grandad said hastily. 'A pony out on grass is no trouble at all. Just don't forget to give her water. And mind that she doesn't get too fat or she could get laminitis. That would cripple her.'

As he rode off, he shouted out of the cab, 'Don't forget the worm dose, Sarah. Then she'll put on the condition.'

I got Bluebell a drink of water and then went inside for my dinner. Mam met me at the door, with a pot of cheese sauce. I love that smell.

'I'm in a hurry. Just give me the sauce with the potatoes.'

'The chops will be done in a minute.'

'I can't wait. Babs is coming down to ride Bluebell.'

The chops sizzled loudly on the pan. 'Sarah, she can't.'

'Grandad said it would be all right to sit up on her for a few minutes every day.'

'Stop shouting . . . now leave your schoolbag into the study. I told you not to dump it where someone might want to sit.'

Catching the bag, I lifted it off the chair and flung it on the tiled floor.

Mam looked at me severely and I glared back. Why does she hate me for wanting to have a good time?

'He also told you to be careful not to spoil her. After all, she is not much more than a baby.'

'She's not a baby. She's a youngster. I've told you before. She may be five years old.'

'Well, a youngster then. Look, Sarah.' Mam's look had softened. 'Training her isn't going to be all fun and games. You'll be learning and she'll be learning. Remember it takes a long time to "make" a horse or a pony but a very short time to spoil one.'

'Grandad said I could ride her.' How come she knew so much about horses all of a sudden!

Mam's voice hardened once more. 'I know this. I'm telling you that you can't sit up on that pony until your Dad comes home. And there is no question of anyone else riding her for the moment.'

I picked up the bag. 'Well, can I put on the headcollar and walk her around?'

'Certainly, but you can start by patting her and talking to her. Be her friend. Come on now and have your dinner.'

Two helpings of potatoes and sauce and two pieces of tart later, I realised that I'd forgotten to eat my lunch in the playground.

Mam didn't mention the washing-up. Hurrying back to my bedroom, I threw off my school uniform and quickly got into my jeans, grabbing the headcollar on the way out.

Bab's head appeared over the ditch and she dropped down into the field. We grinned at each other. She had changed into her jeans too.

'Look.' The apple in her hand was bruised and brown and had a bite taken out of it. 'Where is she?' Babs wanted to give it to her right away.

Bluebell lifted her head when she heard us coming and gave a little whinny of enquiry. Babs gazed at her, goggle-eyed. 'She's gorgeous.' Her voice held a crock of gold in it. You could tell she had never been so excited by anything in her whole life. Her eyeballs were huge. She took a step forward but I said, 'Wait here and I'll lead her over to you. Give me the apple.'

She slowly handed it over and I went up to Bluebell on my own, my left hand stretched out in front with the apple, the right one behind my back holding the headcollar. 'That's a good girl.' Moving slowly, talking quietly to her all the time, hoping she wouldn't run away. Not while Babs was watching. She took a step, then another. 'Good girl.' I handed the apple to her and she nosed it, smelling it, then grazed my palm with her teeth as she munched. She stopped, leaving her muzzle in my palm, then suddenly lifted her head, startled by the sudden loud jangling beside her.

'Don't rush up like that. You'll frighten her.'

'Well, it was my apple, wasn't it?' Babs wouldn't listen, only ran about her, slapping her hard on the neck and rubbing her all over her back, her ears, twirling her tail. Bluebell took no notice and once she had got used to the dangle of the bracelet and the perfume she began grazing again.

Babs stopped. 'Is her eye bursted or what?'

'No. Grandad said she'll grow out of it. I expect her mother gave it to her. But she is a bit dirty. I think we'd better wash her.'

Babs eyes shone. 'Okay. Where will we get the water?'

Luckily Mam was not in the kitchen. We filled a bucket at the sink, making it nice and lukewarm and squirting in lots of washing-up liquid. Then we got a brush, cloths and sponges.

It was a lovely day, sunny with a soft drying breeze. There could be no chance of Bluebell catching cold. She grazed quietly as we worked. That is until we sloshed the water on her. She pulled away from us and stamped her foot. Babs was crouched down at her back legs where she was busily washing. I ran the brush as best I could through her tangled mane, removing clogged mud and washing it down.

As she was drying, we played 'Fetch-the ball' with Bono to pass the time. But there was more to do before we were finished. I took the scissors out of my pocket.

Babs grabbed her mane. 'Let me have a go first.' She started working immediately, chopping away at her mane.

'Now, it's my go.' I cut the fringe over her eyes so she could see better. Then a little bit farther down. It was a good deal shorter now. So was the tail when we were finished. We stood back to look at her.

The scissors clicked in Babs' hand. 'What about her tail? It's still too long.'

'I think we'd better leave it, Babs.'

From behind, 'I'm just going to straighten it another bit.'

We stood back. No doubt about it. After all our hard work she looked much tidier.

But a bell was pealing in the distance and Babs quickly handed me the scissors. 'I have to go now, Sarah.' Her mother was calling her for her tea. Babs told me once that the bell was an antique left to them by her granny. She had a lot of jewels and when she died she was going to leave them to Babs. Babs had got some already but they were in a safe-deposit box in the bank and she had to wear fakes.

'Bye, Babs.'

'Bye, Sarah.'

As we answered each other's calls our voices fell softly on the grass, were blown over hedges and ditches, around the mysterious walls of houses, becoming fainter and fainter. Finally there was no answer. Babs had reached her house.

I patted Bluebell. 'She liked you!'

Bluebell dropped her head into the bucket of fresh drinking water and filtered it through her teeth, blowing bubbles with it while Bono walked around her, wagging his tail, still trying to make friends with her. She lifted her head, water streaming from her mouth each side, ears up, looking towards the gate. Dad had arrived, early, as promised.

Rolling down the car window, he drove through the gate, then stopped. A change came over his face. His eyes were staring in horror at Bluebell.

'What's wrong, Dad?'

'Her mane,' he spluttered. 'You've hogged it!'

'We straightened it,' speaking soothingly to him, trying to calm him down.

'Straightened it! There's nothing left. And you've taken a chunk off her tail.' He glared at me. 'Did you think her mane and tail were just ornaments?'

'Dad!'

'Never do that again. A pony needs a tail to keep off the flies. And a mane is a riding aid. It can help a rider to stay on.'

'It was Babs' fault,' I explained. 'She wouldn't stop cutting. She wouldn't give me the scissors.' At least we hadn't touched the whiskers.

He sighed, 'I've got something for you.' Out of the boot along with his briefcase he took a plastic bag. I opened it. There was a black velvet riding-hat and a new bridle with a small shiny bit and a set of reins.

'Dad, thanks!' I hugged him.

'Better check the hat and see does it fit.'

'How do I tie it?'

He fixed the chinstrap for me. 'Perfect. And after we've exercised Bluebell on the lungeing rein, we can try the bridle on her – the saddler said we can return it if it doesn't fit. But first, I want my tea.' Dad yawned hungrily.

I couldn't wait that long. Feeling the smooth velvet on my head. 'Dad, can I sit up on her back, can I? Now, Dad. Please.'

Dad circled Bluebell's neck with his arm, stroking her.

'Up you go, so.'

You got up on her left side; that much I knew from riding my cousin's pony. First, I leaned across her back, getting her used to my weight, and when she didn't stir I threw my right leg over, Dad gripping it on the far side in case I toppled over. He held the headcollar, his right arm around her neck, patting and talking quietly to her while I sat there. She stirred. 'Hold on tight in case she bucks.' His arm tightened around her neck and I tried clutching the shorn mane. But she stood quietly again, as quiet as a leaf, just moving her tail.

On a pony's back, even a pony the size of Bluebell, you feel high up, like a crow in a nest looking down on the world. Dad, the long two-storey house set into the hill, the trees, gates, fences, bushes, the mountains in the distance, they all looked different. I could see over the wall of the vegetable garden where a rabbit was sneaking out of the cabbages and two magpies were having a scrap with a pigeon on the branch of an ash-tree. From underneath came the delicious feeling of my pony close to me, the strong muscles, the warmth of her soft fur.

Dad patted me on the leg. 'That'll do for now. You can mount her every day while we're breaking her. Let her get used to you on her back.'

I swung down on to the ground again. 'Dad, I'll need a whip.'

'Just be patient.' He sounded tired. 'Money doesn't grow on trees, no matter what you might think.'

Getting her to run around us on the lunge rein was becoming dead easy. 'Whoa, girl.' Dad went over to her. With the headcollar still on her, he took the bridle and very quietly draped the reins over her ears letting it rest on her neck. The bit was still warm from being heated it by the fire and it was smeared with honey. But how were we going to get it into her mouth?

Dad took a book from his pocket and consulted it. 'The secret is to encourage the pony to accept the bit as natural,' he read out. 'I got this book from the library. It has lots of useful tips.'

I felt around her mouth with my hand, remembering what Grandad had done. There was the gap in her teeth at the side and when I pressed at that point, her jaw fell open. Gently Dad eased the bit into her mouth, putting it on her tongue, in the gap between her front and back teeth, on the gums. She made a face as it went in but she took it easily enough and chewed on it as if it was a hard lolly. The rest was simple. The bridle slipped on over her ears and he tied the neckstrap behind her jaw.

The bridle fitted and she looked well with it on her. Dad said, 'When you get in from school every day, put that bridle on her, get her used to the bit.'

Bluebell had accepted the bit without complaint. I was one step nearer to riding her with a bridle and saddle.

That night I couldn't sleep. I'm trotting, cantering and galloping her. I've been selected as a member of the school's riding team to take part in the schools' cross-country competition. Babs has to have a heart and lung transplant. The only way she can have it is by us winning. Already three members of our team have gone and with me last to go, we're down in the score. From her stretcher Babs smiles a cheerful smile and whispers, 'You can do it.' I clench my teeth and set off around the massive course, taking one gianormous jump after the other. And as I fly past the finishing post with the fastest time, pull up on my steaming pony, someone is at my side. It's Trevor, no longer cool, his face full of admiration.

'Are you all right, Sarah? I heard you tossing and turning.'

Open my eyes. 'Yeah. I'm okay, Dad. Goodnight, Dad.'

'Where's the polish? The polish for her hooves.' Babs' eyes were darting about the rain-drenched paddock, now glaring at me. 'You said if I came down we could paint Bluebell's hooves.'

'I know.' If only she would stay and play, even for a little while. We had no playtime today in school on account of the rain.

'Let's go down to the swing.'

'Naw, I don't want to.' She's deliberately looking in the opposite direction, down towards Katie's house, taunting me. Don't plead. Pretend not to care.

'C'mon, Babs. You can have first go. Ah c'mon.' Run off a little, glancing back when no footsteps follow, slowing down, drifting back to her, even though the last thing you want is for her to suspect how badly you need her to stay, show her the power she has over you.

'Mam wouldn't give me the polish. She said we'd only make a mess.'

'Then there's nothing to do.'

'We'll get Bono to root a rabbit's burrow. Maybe we'll find some rabbits sleeping there.' Delay her going, even for a little while.

Her mouth curled on both sides. 'No, I don't want to. Let's go down to Katie's house.'

'I can't. I must wait for Dad.'

'Well, then, can I have a go on Bluebell? Please.' She says it in a babyish, pleading sort of voice. Any minute now the nudge will change to a shove.

'Her back is too soft. And anyway, Mam and Dad won't allow it.'

'Then how come you're allowed?' The scowl was back.

'I'm not allowed until Dad comes home. And don't walk so near her back legs. She could kick you.' If only she'd stop asking.

'Sarah, please, or I won't be your friend. Please.'

I hated it when she was like that, breaking down my wall with those hardening green eyes. I glanced over towards the windows of the house, caught the flutter of a curtain.

'No, Babs. You might spoil her.'

Babs had a big puss on. 'Can I have a ride when your Dad comes home?'

'Dad won't allow it.'

She moved away. 'I think I'd better be going to Katie's.' She climbed up slowly on to the ditch and lingered on the ridge, her back to me, twiddling a long blade of grass in her fingers, while I tried not to look at her and kept rubbing Bluebell, glancing up through my eyelashes every now and then.

She said again, 'I have to go now.' I said nothing. 'Can you come down to Katie's?'

My pony's muzzle is soft and comforting. 'I can't. I'm waiting for Dad.'

'I have to go now.'

'Okay,' I heard myself say. 'See you.'

She moved slowly down off the bank on to the far side. Half way down the field, she turned. Then she walked on, still looking backwards. She reached the five-bar gate and put her hands on the top bar getting ready to climb it, out of sight.

At my call she came running to the ditch.

'Will you be down tomorrow?'

Her face fell, as if she had lost something. 'Okay.'

I went back to patting Bluebell. For the first time ever, I hadn't pleaded with Babs to stay. But she was going to be in a very bad mood.

3 SERVANT TO A PONY

Winter's cold lick clings to the wind, driving swallows low and gusting the pony's tail between her legs. Yet, like a cat, a creamy yellow light has crept into the day. And in the garden the flowering currant bushes are blooming. And all over the valley, grass is shading to watery green, while lambs' voices carry up in a song that drowns the little robin in the thin bushes.

Having Bluebell has changed my life. I am now what I've always wanted to be: a servant to a pony.

On Saturday Dad announced, 'We'll take the pony out the road on the long reins.'

We harnessed Bluebell in Grandad's contraption. The wide belt around her waist tied with binder twine – so as to accustom her to the feel of the saddle later on – had two copper curtain rings attached through which the long ropes fed on to the bridle for steering.

She walked smartly up the road, making little noise. As it was my job to stay in front, I had to run. Dick, our neighbour, was digging in his garden, his pair of brown and white ducks pouncing on any moving creatures as he turned up the earth. When he saw us, Robbie, his sheepdog, fired friendly barks carelessly into the sky.

Bluebell pulled up and put her head in over the hedge. Dick patted her with his big lumpy hand. She nuzzled him. 'Good pony,' he spoke kindly to her. 'I always wanted a pony like you to put under a small trap.' Turning to look at me cheerfully, 'I'd swop you Robbie and the ducks for her.'

'No way,' I said.

He looked at her again and sighed. Telling us to wait, he went into the house and came back with a long whip like you see in the circus.

'I kept it after my pony died,' he said. 'You have it now. Just twirl it over her head.' He flicked it like the ring-master. 'That will help her know when you want her to go on.'

'Thanks, Dick.' Dad cracked it behind Bluebell and she walked on.

I heard the noise first. Round the bend trundled a huge yellow earth-digger and it filled up the width of the road as it approached, shaking the hill and sky. At my frantic waving, the driver slowed down and pulled in as best he could. Bluebell stopped, head in the air. 'Go on.' The whip was useless. Whinnying loudly, she whirled about, catching Dad by surprise. He stumbled over the ropes, just stopping himself from falling flat. His face was red and wet, hair flopping about his ears. Bluebell was all sweat and wrapped in white ropes, but she looked mighty and we were powerless.

There was nothing else for it. Walking quietly up to her, I gripped her by the headcollar. 'Steady.' She jerked her head, bumping me with her shoulder, but my hand had a firm hold. Dad was shouting something. Steady. Now, walk on. She took a small step forward. And another. With me leading her, she marched past the huge digger.

'Good girl.' Running on again, just in time. A haulage truck rattled around the corner. Barely slowing, even though I was signalling madly to the driver. No need to worry. Bluebell stood calmly to let it pass and walked confidently ahead.

And then, for no reason at all that anyone could see, she halted in the middle of the road. Dad was urging her on, but she just stood there, head down, sniffing the pond of water. Then Dad laughed in relief. 'It's her reflection. She's seeing a pal down under.'

After making a big ripple she stepped daintily on.

On our way back, Dick leaned over the hedge and

offered a raw potato to Bluebell. She sniffed it, then nibbled it out of his hand, making clinking noises with the bit. He wiped some of the green slime from her mouth. 'That froth is a good sign. It shows she is working the bit. Atta pony. She's very quiet.' He beamed at her.

'Remarkably quiet,' Dad agreed.

This was my chance. 'Dad, can I ride her on my own today in the big field?' That's the field opposite the paddock on the other side of the driveway.

'Not yet, Sarah.' He nodded goodbye to Dick.

Back home, Dad said he would walk me around the field. We untied the long ropes and I hopped up on her back, Dad with his hand on the headcollar underneath the bridle and reins. All is calm and restful up here on her warm moving body.

Then a rabbit leaped from the tuft of grass at Bluebell's feet. Before I could steady her, she broke free of Dad's grip and bolted, quickly settling into a full gallop.

'Hold on, Sarah! Hold on!'

Bounding, bounding, we galloped away up the big field, Dad still holding on to the headcollar, being pulled along, trying to close in on us, arms in the air, legs stretched like a giant's, while I gripped in my legs for dear life, holding tight on to the reins, yelling at him to let go. Then I stopped: something unreal had happened. Instead of bumping up and down, I was moving with the pony, hardly bouncing at all. The two of us were moving like one.

I yelled again at Dad, telling him it was okay. It was exciting travelling so fast and I was not afraid any more. I shouted and slapped the reins off my helmet. Wind rushed through my hair. I didn't want her to stop. I wanted her to go faster!

Dad let go, swaying helplessly, sinking down into the grass and we continued on our own.

When Bluebell finally started to slow down, I tried to urge her on again without result. 'Come on, Dad. Get her to do it again. Dad!'

But Dad had gone into the house. He'd had enough of Bluebell for one day.

'Hi!' How long had Babs been standing up on the ditch, watching what was happening.

'Did you see me cantering?'

'Sort of,' she shrugged.

'Get me a stick. A big one.' Dad had taken the whip.

Babs grinned, friendly-like, and I knew she was in a better mood. We were in for a bit of fun. Climbing into the hedge she broke off a leafy elderberry branch. Shook it into the pony's face.

I cantered Bluebell up the field, Babs behind us waving the bush. Bono joined in the chase, barking with pleasure.

'Sarah!'

With a screech, Babs stopped running. 'It's your Mam.'

'Put down that bush.'

Still grinning, Babs dropped it.

We went over to Mam at the gate, Bono carrying the bush in his mouth behind us. She looked big and grim. Only now, on Bluebell's back I'm as big as her.

'What would your parents say?'

'It was Sarah's idea.' The smile had gone from Babs' face. I thought, 'She's afraid Mam will tell on her and she'll get into trouble,' so she slips the blame on me.

I tried to explain. 'She wouldn't go for me.' But Mam turned on me fiercely. 'I warned you about ruining her. You're the one who's really responsible.'

'I wouldn't have to gallop if you bought me a saddle. I could trot.'

'The pony isn't ready yet for a saddle. Anyway you have a saddle, the one Grandad gave you.'

'The stuffing is coming out of it! And it's a donkey's saddle. Dick said so.'

Babs giggled. Then Mam got really mad. she went through the whole rigmarole about all the gear I have in the house and hardly ever use, the ballet clothes, the gym clothes, the Irish dancing costume Granny got made for me years ago, the piano, the violin. And now I wanted a new saddle.

I watched Bluebell putting away the whole of a bucket of water. It's better not to listen to Mam when she gives out, so as to save your ears the damage. With Dad it's different. He 'docks' points off. I don't know yet what the points are for, but it's pretty serious.

Babs was really worried, until Mam told her she wouldn't tell her mother this time.

Straightway, after Mam went back into the house, Babs wanted to have a go at riding Bluebell. 'Give me a leg up.'

Bluebell stirred and she fell over on the grass. We broke our sides laughing while she lay there. 'Put me up again.'

'No, Babs. Let's go to the ranch house.'

Our ranch house in Clinton's bushes is soft and cosy with moss. We sat there in its secret warmth, hearing Babs' small brother calling her while we talked about our plans and about Katie Ruten Spillane in the old mill.

'Katie doesn't like you.'

'Why?'

'Because you have podgy cheeks.'

'But I haven't.'

'I know.' She looked sorrowfully at the heap of leaves we had gathered to try and light a fire by rubbing two stones together.

'Let me have a go.' I took them from her.

'Do you like her?' she said, ''Cos I don't.'

'I don't like her either.' I struck the two stones together. 'I hate her.'

It was teatime and as I ran through the fields for home I remembered to collect the bridle from where we had thrown it in the field. Bluebell was grazing nearby.

'Come here, Bluebell, good girl.' I suppose I wanted to say 'Sorry' as I walked up to her as usual and, if she let me, sit on her back.

She lifted her head. Then suddenly, ears back, she came charging towards me, only to sidestep at the last minute. She circled me threateningly, giving small buck leaps and kicking out with hooves that came dangerously close, once grazing my arm. Then she took off again, bucking and plunging around the field.

Dick was digging our garden and he joined me at the railings. His blue eyes were shining as they followed her antics. 'She's only playing. Her kicks are aimed to miss you. Let her run until she gets tired.' He leaned on his spade and waited while I went back to her.

With Dick there I didn't feel so afraid. Going up behind her I shouted at her and chased after her, flapping my arms about. She ran for a while, then slowed down and stood snorting loudly, eyeing our approach. Ignoring me she went for the potato in Dick's outstretched hand. Patting her neck while she ate, Dick spoke quietly to her,' Oh, there's a good pony,' reaching for her bob. But quick as a wink she swung away, leaving a tuft of hair in his hands. Fast, but not fast enough, for Dick reached out and grabbed her by the tail. She stopped, looking back with a surprised look then stood quietly while his hand moved up along her back. His arm was circling her neck.

'Thanks, Dick. But it's too late for me to ride her.'

He stroked her, let her go again.

In bed, through the living-room partition, I could hear Mam and Dad talking.

'That pony is getting too strong for her. She's running wild.' Mam's voice was high-pitched. 'I know Sarah is going to get hurt. She's your daughter too and you don't care. We should get rid of that pony. I tell you, I can't stand it!'

'Shush, Ann.' Dad's voice was low. 'Riding bareback is great practice for her. It'll make a rider of her and it is quite safe in the field. Soon she'll be able to use the saddle and she'll have a lot more control. There's no need to get hysterical.'

'But she doesn't know how to manage that pony! An inexperienced rider on an inexperienced pony!'

'Maybe,' Dad yawned loudly, 'Maybe she should have a riding-lesson.'

Dad put his newspaper beside him on the couch. 'Look Sarah, I didn't get a new saddle. Grandad's one will have to do you for the time being. New saddles are expensive. Anyway, it's time you yourself did something.'

He sounded tired, probably after his chase with Bluebell yesterday. Or else maybe he got the blood samples mixed up today at work and got into trouble. I mean it can happen. Dad works in a hospital laboratory. He takes blood

from patients and tests it for diseases and stuff: a kind of
Dracula. 'Bluebell's hooves are curling up fast. Find out
who the farrier is and contact him.' He closed his eyes and
put his head back on the chair. 'And don't wait for me to do
it.'

The farrier: that was Niall's dad. I rang, hoping Niall
would answer, never having made a business call before.
But it was Mr. Hickey himself.

'This is Sarah Kleptoria Quinn from Tooten Hill. My
pony needs shoes.'

'Right-o, Sarah,' his voice sounded as if he knew me
already. 'I have a few horses to do in the Curragh in the
morning. But I'll be over later. What time do you get in
from school?'

I was home before he came and opened the gate for him to
drive through. Luckily Bluebell was easy to catch and I led
her over to him. He spoke to her in a low murmur while she
smelled at the black leather apron he took from the boot of
his car to tie around his middle. In the centre of the apron
was a worn patch the shape of a horseshoe. 'Whoa, girl.' He
stooped and with a hand the size of a basket lifted up her
foot until it rested on his apron, then got to work with his
rasp. I held her by the headcollar in case she moved and
Mam fed her fists of green grass. We chatted all the time
while he worked – Mam called him Willie. I told him how
she was a present from Grandad.

He rested for a moment, holding the hoof on his thigh. 'A
grand quiet little mare.'

'Grandad says there's a touch of Connemara in her.'

'Aye. There's a few grand little shows you could bring her
to. They have musical chairs competitions and other little
things.' His rasp sounded again. That hoof dropped and he
was working on the next one. Bluebell munched away,
showing no nervousness or wanting to get away. At last he
straightened his back.

'Her hooves are pared. But I won't be able to shoe her this time. I've no shoes small enough to fit her.'

'Will I check?' I rushed to the boot of his car to make sure and picked out a small shiny one. Mr Hickey took it from me, measured it against her hoof to show me, and handed it back. 'Fix that above your door for luck.'

Then suddenly, in an offhand voice, Mam was asking about a second-hand saddle.

Resting his hands on his hips, Willie said, 'I can get you one. It'll be a right one. You can get cheap foreign ones but they're not right at all.'

'When can you get it?' I couldn't keep my leg from hammering off the gravel.

He looked thoughtful. 'I'll be travelling up to the North of Ireland soon and I'll get you an English saddle. It won't be too dear. Maybe a hundred pounds or less. Not the greatest, but it would do you for a start.'

As he drove away Mam muttered, 'The gear is costing more than the pony.'

'Tack, not gear, Mam.' I felt like hugging her.

She muttered again, heading for the house.

'Mam,' I called after her, 'I don't need to go to summer camp this year. That will save some money. And I have my birthday money.'

'You'd need a few more birthdays,' she said sourly.

When Dad came home, we put Grandad's saddle on Bluebell for the first time. She stood quietly enough as he tightened the girth, then loosened it again. He was looking anxiously at her face. 'I'm not sure how tight this should be on her.' He started to tighten it again. But she seemed to have got fatter. 'Place your foot in the stirrup,' holding her while I swung up into it. The saddle slipped right around. Dad let out a grunt and this time he tied it tightly. 'She was holding her breath, the rascal,' he gasped. One leg was longer than the other in the stirrups but I balanced myself nicely. I rode slowly up the field in a straight line.

'Mam, watch me.' She had come out of the house and was standing with Dad under the oak-tree. I faced Bluebell down towards them again. Without words, just by looking at their faces, anyone could see that to them Bluebell was the cutest pony in the whole world. I only wished that Grandad could see us. First I got Bluebell to trot. Up, down, rise and fall like my cousins told me, missed a few. Not very comfortable, bouncing up and down, and Bluebell was swishing her tail, opening her mouth, but I was getting the hang of it. Cantering was easier; you just stay put in the saddle. I urged her on into a fast gallop. Turning at the top we came back down, breezing along, barely touching the ground.

'Don't go so hard!'

Taking a hand off the reins I waved. Now I know how Our Lord felt when he rode the donkey into Jerusalem.

I wasn't supposed to go out on my own but that ride on Bluebell filled me with confidence and next morning, before going to school, I rode her again. We walked around at first. 'Go on, Bluebell,' tipping her with the stick. Suddenly she took off, rearing and bucking up the field, and at the five-barred gate she swerved and threw me, then stood boldly looking at me. I crept back into the house and left the tack in the utility room. It was not a good start to the day. And things got worse.

At school I told Babs that I might soon take Bluebell to a show. Suddenly she was in a very bad mood, shouting, 'Get lost! I'm playing with Katie.'

'What's up?' Niall was passing by on his way to fetch a football off the grass.

'Babs told Katie I hated her. I said I didn't, but Katie won't believe me. They're telling lies about me.'

Niall bent his arm. 'Feel that muscle,' he said proudly. 'I don't like those two. Want me to give them something to think about?'

'Yeah, well, no thanks, Niall. It's okay. Really. You'd only get into trouble.'

Then I heard Trevor asking Susan if she was going to the disco in the hall. Of course I'm not allowed to go. I'm not allowed do anything only ride a mad pony that's going to kill me!

Back home, I threw my bag on the floor and slammed the doors, loudly.

'Babs says her dad is buying a whole field of ponies.' Voice low, simmering, like the cheese sauce Mam's stirring.

'So what?'

She took a step back as I screamed at her, 'Don't stick up for her. She's telling lies all the time. She said she was getting a pony at Smithfield on Sunday.

'But her mam told me they weren't going to Smithfield Horse Fair. This Sunday. Or any other Sunday!' The school bus had broken down and she had given me a lift home in the car. That was when I had talked to her.

'Never mind,' Mam's voice was mild. 'Why don't you get ready and go out on your pony as soon as you've had your dinner.'

'Bluebell!' Like a slap, the memory of the morning struck me. Trying to control her and she in that mad bucking and rearing mood, meeting the hard ground. No siree. Not again.

'Come and eat your dinner.' She put it out on the plate.

'I don't want it. I'm not hungry. I'm sick of cheese sauce!'

Suddenly Mam crossed the floor to me. Silently she put her arms around me, gave me a long hug. There was a sigh, from which one of us I'm not sure.

'Don't forget,' her voice was soft. 'You're growing bigger and stronger too, just like she is. See,' she held me at arm's length. 'You're past my shoulder now.'

'Okay,' I pushed away my plate. 'I'll ride Bluebell when Dad comes home and do my homework now.'

Dad caught her and together we saddled her up. She walked nicely around the paddock, head into the wind. So far so good. I turned her down into the big field for a gallop. But as we cantered through the gateway, she swerved to the left, then dashed away in a mad gallop up the middle, eating up the ground while I clung on, right foot out of the stirrup, grasping for her mane. I slid down her neck, nearer the ground that was shaking under her strong hooves. One big buck and I hit it shoulder first. I lay there, hearing myself gasping. My thumb and shoulder hurt bad enough to be broken.

Dad was beside me, asking me if I was all right. Where was I sore? He felt my hand and my leg. 'You're okay.'

I stumbled to my feet, looked around me distractedly.

But Dad was grinning at me. 'That was a good tumble you got. You were a great little rider to stay on. At least she pulled up when you fell. That's a good sign.' Bluebell was grazing innocently beside us.

'You'd better get up again.' She let him catch her. I hung back.

'I don't want to. She's dangerous.'

But Dad assured me, 'She's just a lively little pony that needs plenty of riding. I'm going to lunge her first. She's too full of beans.'

Bluebell kicked and bucked and made rude noises going around in the circle. When she got tired, Dad put me astride her again.

I walked her around, clutching the reins tightly, afraid she was going to throw me again, and after a short time pulled up. 'Will you untack for me, Dad? I have to see Babs about some geography we have to learn off.'

Dad took the reins from me and frowned. 'Bluebell needs more work-outs than she's getting.'

'I'll ride her again when I come down,' I promised.

Babs might be pleased to see me if Katie was not around to play with her. I rang the doorbell. She stood in the narrow opening looking as pleased as if I was extra homework and there was a fantastic programme on telly she wanted to watch.

'Hi.' She waited there, still in her school uniform.

'Can you come up to play?'

'Won't you be riding Bluebell?'

'Yeah. But you can watch.'

'I can't. Mam has my dinner ready.'

'Can I come in and wait for you?'

'No.'

On the way home, the shouts and whistles of Babs and Katie echoed after me through the fields.

Surprise! The space beside Katie is vacant today – Babs had an appointment with the dentist.

In the playground, she sat on the bench beside me. Even if it is Katie, she's better than no one at all.

'Can I come over to see Bluebell?' Her voice was hopeful. 'I ride my cousins' ponies when we go to Kerry.'

'Okay.' A small bit of clear blue sky was showing overhead between the clouds. 'Do you want to play tag? You can be on.'

We got up off the bench and played together, all big break too, and on the way home sat together on the bus.

After school, just as I was finishing my dinner, Katie knocked on the door. She was dressed in her jeans and runners and I changed quickly into mine.

Bluebell eyed her brown plaits and tried to nip them. 'She's lovely!'

'You can sit up on her if you like.' I gave her a leg up and she sat there. 'Babs said you don't like me.'

'And she told me you didn't like me.'

Bluebell gave a slight start. 'Hi!' There was Babs looking down at us from the top of the ditch. She slithered down and Katie and I watched her in silence. For once I was not happy to see her.

'Can I have a go too?' Her voice was soft but threatening.

Katie got down and together we helped Babs up. 'Let me have a go on my own.' she pushed our hands away.

'Don't, Babs. Dad won't allow it.'

The old familiar scowl returned.

'Okay. You can just walk her around.' Grinning, Babs walked Bluebell a short distance.

'You'd better come back now. Mam might be watching.'

'No!' She shook the reins. 'I want to trot. Gee up there.'

She was shouting and kicking with her heels. Bluebell responded. Now Babs was screaming, bumping up and down, yanking at the reins. But Bluebell kept going. Then turning, she sped down the hill at breakneck speed. With a scream Babs fell to the ground under the pony's hooves and lay there without moving.

Katie and I ran across.

'She just got a bit of a fright. We'd better get her out of the field in case Mam hears.' I put my hand over Babs' mouth to muffle her screeches. She and Katie limped off, one supporting the other. Even in the distance I could hear Babs crying about her sore head.

I stared at my pony, at the ugly face and two funny eyes. Babs had been my special friend. Now I had none. She probably would never speak to me again. Only for Bluebell we'd still be friends.

'Just go away.' I raised my hand and, with a surprised look, Bluebell ambled off.

That night in bed, only one thing helped me to go to sleep. I remembered how, in the ranch house, Babs had told me that she and her small brother Jack were discussing their friends. Babs asked Jack who he preferred.

'Katie or Sarah?'

'Sarah, of course.'

When Jack asked Babs she answered, 'Sarah, of course.'

That was a miracle.

4 CELBRIDGE SHOW

'Hey, that poem is good!' Niall, leaning over my side of the desk. 'I wish I could write like that.'

The poem is about looking into a pool and seeing yourself and then disappearing.

I looked over at Trevor, hoping he'd hear, hoping he'd ask to read my poem. He looked across. Shoved back his sleek coif to show one eyebrow. He looks so cute when he does that. Smiled, then returned to Susan, who's leaning back and swishing her golden hair in his face. 'Trevor! You didn't!' That high-pitched girly laugh really set my teeth watering.

Niall tapped my arm. 'Did you hear what I said? There's a show on in Celbridge. Trevor and I are going to it. Will you be bringing your pony?'

'A show? What do you have to do at it?'

'Well,' a small knot appeared on his forehead as he explained, 'you jump over a set of jumps and if you don't knock any of them, or don't fall off, you get a clear round and win a rosette. Get the idea? We were there last year. I won two rosettes.' He nodded with his biro in Trevor's direction. 'He has a very good pony. Grade A. He won six rosettes.'

'A grey day pony?' I asked.

'Yeah, Grade A,' he went on, not realising my stupid mistake. 'That means he has a very high number of points, collected from winning at the different shows. Mine is Grade C. Well, he was when we got him. He's probably only Grade D now. What's your pony? Is she graded?

'No. I told you she's never won anything or never been to

a show. She's too young. She wouldn't be jumping.'

'Well, there are other competitions.'

Trevor was smiling at me. 'So you've got a new pony, Sarah? Must see her some time. Do you hunt her? It's good fun.' He turned away again.

Clearing my throat I answered loudly, 'I don't think so. She's only a youngster.'

Trevor shrugged and Susan said something to him and tittered. Babs, she *would* have to, came over with Katie to see what was going on.

Niall said, 'You're lucky. I'd love a young pony that I could train myself instead of an old pony that's going nowhere. But Dad reckons if he was good enough for my brother, he's good enough for me. It's not fair.'

Leaning on our desk, Babs said, 'Me and Sarah were training her, weren't we, Sarah? It was brilliant.'

I looked at her, wondering what she was up to and saw her eyeing Susan. She doesn't like Susan either.

'Yeah,' I said.

Niall said, 'I bet you fell off.'

'Cop on! No, I didn't!' Babs hit him on the shoulder and he clouted her back, grinning, bending his arm at her to show his muscle.

She hit him again and dodged away from him. 'Sure I didn't, Sarah?'

'No.' I hoped God wasn't listening.

'I hope you can go to the Show,' Niall said again when she moved away. 'It'll be good fun.'

Wet sunshine, Dandelions glittered in the pony's paddock and down below in the big field, short grasses waved soft and green in the breeze.

I tacked up Bluebell, waiting for Dad to come home so that I could go out riding. I wanted him to hear the news about the Show. I hoped he'd agree.

His car was at the gate. I waited at the fence as he parked

and walked towards me, bushy red hair standing on his head, smiling.

'Hi, Dad.' It's not easy to talk when your teeth are clamped shut. I opened the chinstrap on my crash helmet. 'Mrs Davis, our Principal, asked me in the playground if I was going to the Show at St Blaize's. It's in aid of the school. I told her that I might not be able, that Bluebell was still only a youngster. But please, can I?'

Words tumbled out. 'Niall Hickey is going. His pony is only the same height as Bluebell. And Grandad did say she would win a class, no bother. And Dad, please can I? Dad! Are you listening to me, Dad?'

But he was just standing there staring at the pony, almost as if he had never seen her before.

I waved the whip in front of his eyes. 'The Show, Dad. Can I go to the Show?'

He broke out of his trance. 'The Show? . . . I don't see.' He stopped and took a deep breath. 'I don't see how you can. It must be seven miles away. We'd have to walk there.'

'Bluebell would be well able.' I patted her warm neck.

He was smiling again. 'I know. But what about your Dad?'

'You could wear your runners . . . she might win a rosette.'

'She might,' he said thoughtfully. 'I suppose there's no harm in finding out if there's a competition for her.' Then he looked carefully at me. 'But let's be clear about one thing – she is young and you can't expect too much from her yet.'

'I know that, Dad.' But I knew what he was really thinking. How could that skinny little pony with the spiky coat win anything? Well, Dad didn't know what I knew: Bluebell was a winning pony.

'Dad, if there is a competition for her, can I go?'

'When is it on?'

'Sunday week.'

He said abruptly, 'Then you have only a week to get her ready.'

'Dad!'

'Look, I can't promise for definite. We'll have to see how much she improves and that is largely up to you. So you'd better start right now. But maybe I'd better lunge her first. You can get the rope while I'm changing.'

After lungeing her, this time with me sitting on her back as she circled, he unfastened the rope on the bridle and said, 'Remember, flying about the field on her is no use. You must school her, trot her in a circle and a figure eight over and over again, getting her to move freely and smoothly from walk to trot – especially on the trot – and only then should you work at canter. That's how you'll make her mouth and gain control and get her to move with suppleness.'

'I know, Dad, I know. I read the book too.'

After he left, Bluebell and I worked on the circle and the figure eight, turning and twisting. Very soon we both needed a break badly. I opened the gate down into the big field and we got in a bit of chasing. Chasing through the fields is far more exciting and Bluebell enjoys it too.

It was Mam who thought of asking Babs to come to the Show with us. I couldn't wait until next day to ask her at school so I rang her.

Babs said, 'I don't mind,' like as if she didn't care whether she came or not. But next day she let me join in the games, although Katie did not look too happy about it.

After school every day, I managed to fit in some training. The more I rode Bluebell the more we were getting to understand each other. She was obedient and did what I asked her to do, most times. But she still clung to that one bad habit of running away. She had developed quite a trick of racing straight on when I'd ask her to turn and by putting up her head she was able to avoid the bit so that I couldn't steer her, even with her head twisted almost right around.

'Cheeky pony.' A slap from the whip made her buck and go flying away again. I was learning to grip on much better and didn't fall off like before.

One other thing I forgot to mention. Two days before the show, Niall gave me a present. Well, it wasn't exactly for me. 'I've got something here you're going to need.' While Sir was out of the room he put his head in under the desk and rooted around for his satchel. 'Is Bluebell hairy? Thought so. All ponies are hairy at this time of year. Seeing as you're going to the show, you'll have to brush her and plait and comb her mane and tail. Otherwise the judges won't look at her.' He pulled out a plastic bag. 'You can have it. It's my old grooming kit. I just got a new one.'

'Thanks, Niall.' I looked inside and took out a steel comb.

'That's for her mane,' he said. 'You brush her with this first,' showing me a coarse brush. 'And this fine one is the body brush.' It was full of brown pony hairs. 'Sorry, I meant to clean it. But, don't worry, there's no lice in it or anything.'

'Gee, thanks. I'll keep them safe for you, just in case you lose the new set.'

'They're for keeps. Just don't tell Babs where you got them. She's a pain.'

'Actually,' I pushed the grooming kit into the bottom of my bag, 'she's very nice at the moment.'

Niall grunted.

'It's no use, Babs. She'll never win a prize looking like that.'

Babs stopped brushing and giggled. We had been brushing and combing Bluebell for hours. We had even plaited her mane but the plaits kept coming out and she still had the appearance of a hedgehog. It was a bit disappointing.

'What'll we do?' Babs whacked the dandruff out of the

brush, sending it showering into the air.

'We'll get Hermencita. She really knows how to make up a pony for a show.' Hermencita went to Pony Club and kept her pony in a garden. She lived opposite the school.

She opened the door, looking real cool in long skin-tight navy jodhpurs, with a blue striped shirt.

'Wait here. Do you mind?'

We played with her wolfhound, Roisin, until she came back wearing her wax jacket.

'Hop in, kids.'

The alarm sounded as she put the key in the door of a gleaming new red car.

'Is it yours?' Babs' mouth was wide.

We both sat into the back seat and we whizzed up the hill. 'Yes. Got it for my birthday.'

Babs whispered to me, 'I'm getting one of them when I'm seventeen, my Dad said.'

Letting out a whinny of curiosity, Bluebell ambled over for a closer look at the newcomer and Hermencita jerked her head away to avoid a friendly lick. 'Is she graded?'

'No,' Babs said. 'Is yours?'

'He's Grade C. I'm expecting to upgrade him this year. Got the rubber bands? Just pass them to me, will you?'

Babs got there first. She dangled them from her fingers, red, yellow and blue ones.

'Got any black?'

'No. Would a bicycle tube do?' Grandad had told me you could make elastic bands from an old tube, but Hermencita interrupted, 'Got a steel comb?'

'Yeah, sure,' I handed her the one Niall gave me and she began combing the mane slowly, carefully, parting it with her long red nails. 'Where did your pony come from?'

'From a bog.'

'Yeah,' added Babs. How come Babs always had to butt into a conversation, especially when she didn't know what we were talking about.

'Her mane is uneven.' Hermencita was tugging at it, pulling chunks out of it. Then suddenly she stopped. A small shiver passed through her. 'What's that?' Pointing at Bluebell's flank.

'It's a kind of itch.' I flicked some away with my hand and quickly she drew back. 'Grandad put stuff on it, it's nearly cleared up now. She loves scratching herself on the gooseberry bushes.'

'Where can I wash my hands?' Hermencita was biting her lips. 'That's sweet-itch. It's infectious and contagious.'

She waved to us from the driveway as she drove away.

'What's wrong with her?' Babs said grinning.

'Dunno.' I picked up the steel comb. 'We'll just continue on ourselves and we won't bother with the tail, just put a tail bandage on it.'

Mam arrived to help and began plaiting. But because the mane was short and springy, the bands kept loosening and some plaits stuck up, some down.

Mam sighed. 'Her face looks even more baldy. Maybe we don't need to plait her at all.'

'Mam! Niall said that unless she's plaited, the judges won't even look at her!'

She handed me back the comb. 'I think I'll go in and get your riding gear ready. You have to try on that jacket Auntie May sent you. It might look better when it's pressed and I'll do that now.'

Babs and I carried on until Babs started blowing on her fingers. 'They're getting sore.' She made a face.

'Yeah, so are mine. Bluebell, stop shaking your head!' A few more plaits came tumbling loose.

When Babs had gone home I went inside and, before my tea, tried on my riding clothes, dressing in my cousin's old beige jodhpurs, white shirt, the yellow tie that belonged to Dad, pulling on the black boots. Mam buttoned up the navy riding-jacket, handed me my new helmet. After examining me, she stood back. She was smiling.

'Have a look at yourself.'

I twirled in front of the long mirror in the hallway and what I saw made me laugh and set my leg hopping.

Dad said, 'You look terrific. A real show rider.'

But Mam was still talking to herself. 'I'll turn up the jodhpurs, maybe turn up the sleeves of the coat. Don't you feel those boots a bit big on you?'

'Don't worry, Mam, the judges will be looking at Bluebell, not me.'

'Wear my thick woolly socks,' Dad joked.

I pulled back the curtains to let the sun in and quickly slipping on my jeans ran out to Bluebell. Some of her plaits had to be redone where she scratched them the night before, and I wrapped her tail in the yellow bandage to keep it neat until we got to the showgrounds. My tack needed a final polish to bring out the sheen.

'Sarah, better have your breakfast. It's nearly time to get moving.'

Dad was lacing his runners, he had already eaten. I nibbled at a few cornflakes, then dashed off to get dressed. Back in the kitchen, Mam was standing by to brush my hair. 'It would look nice plaited with yellow ribbons.'

'Good luck!' Mam and Dick stood watching us until we went around the bend, Bluebell moving quickly down the hill on her small hooves, Dad striding along beside us. Being Sunday morning, the road was quiet. Not even a dog barked as we walked along, keeping in by the grass verge. A football thudded at the back of O'Donnell's house but Bluebell took no notice.

Once she got out on the open road, Bluebell made fast progress despite her short dainty steps. As Dad had planned we took the quieter back road around by the demesne. The breeze was to our backs and the clouds sailed happily by overhead. Bluebell, with her nose almost stitched to Dad's shoulder, was nearly hidden behind him, nuzzling him whenever he slowed down. We passed farmhouses and cottages and big green wheat fields and she kept pushing on over the humpbacked canal bridge and the railway bridge. Even the mighty diesel-engined train that roared past underneath, she took no more notice of than of a gust of wind.

'We're doing well.' Dad sounded calm. We barely spoke at all or made any noise as we went along, him with his runners and Bluebell without shoes.

The car horn behind us was Mam with the picnic. Bluebell grazed on the grassy margin – when she wasn't gobbling my sandwiches. Babs would laugh. Suddenly I remembered, 'Mam, you forgot Babs! Where is she?'

'She didn't turn up.'

'Mam, I told her you would pick her up!'

Mam shrugged. 'Pity you didn't tell me.'

On the road again I forgot about Babs. Not too far to go now. A loudspeaker sounded and Bluebell's ears went up. 'I think we're nearly there, Dad.'

At the gate, a man waved us in. Mam ran to meet us. 'There's one class to go before yours, so you've plenty of time,' pointing to where she was parked. I rode on down the big field with Dad holding the reins, meeting other horses being walked and trotted about by their riders, weaving our way through tents and people. The loudspeaker sounded loudly and Bluebell jerked at the bit and let out an enormous whinny that sent a mighty shiver through her whole body, shaking like a rat in Bono's mouth. Dad led her past the horse-boxes, telling me to pet her, but I decided to keep my two hands tight on the reins.

'Can you hurry?' Mam was nervous. She fetched my yellow gloves and attached to my lapel a red rose from Dick's glasshouse.

Up in the saddle, gripping the reins in one hand I adjusted my stirrups, then straightened up at the sound of someone calling my name. Niall and Trevor trotted over to us on their ponies. 'Your pony is lovely.' Niall's face bulged out under a small helmet. His pony had brown and white markings.

'What's his name again?' Trevor, tall in the saddle, smiling, resting a hand on his pony's neck.

'It's a she! Bluebell.' Trevor's pony was bigger, with hooves like turnips.

Then Niall said, 'Would you like to ride around with us?'

We rode off, Bluebell and me in the middle. In the company of the other two ponies, her confidence returned and she settled down to a more relaxed pace. I was enjoying myself too.

I turned to Niall on my right and asked him, 'Is that Teabag?'

'Yes,' Niall patted his pony. 'He's brilliant. I think he's not old at all.'

The other pony's name was Spinifex. 'Just call him Hayseed,' drawled Trevor. 'Everybody does.'

Hayseed had a headband full of red rosettes. 'We got them in the clear round jumping.' Trevor adjusted one that had fallen over his pony's eye. 'Every time you have a clear you get a red rosette.'

'I fell off,' Niall said. 'So they wouldn't give me one.' He didn't look too worried. The announcement over the loudspeaker was clear and I turned my pony about. 'My competition is coming up next. I'd better go.'

'Good luck,' Trevor raised his hand in salute.

'Leave a few rosettes for us,' Niall shouted.

A small girl pointed at Bluebell as we passed. 'Oh look. What a beautiful pony.' I sat straighter in the saddle.

Dad came rushing up and grabbed the bridle. 'Ring 5. this way. The beginners' class.' He led us to the roped area where other ponies and their riders had gathered. I rode in and walked around with them. Two people standing in the middle of the ring were beckoning to us.

'Trot on,' said the man in the round black hat. I urged Bluebell forward but she was distracted, looking around her for Teabag and Hayseed. She took a few steps, then stopped, lifted her tail. A tap of the whip made no difference. The other competitors were bunched up behind Bluebell and all stopped and waited until she finished a very long piddle.

'Trot on,' the judge, hands behind his back, was bending to the lady in the headscarf. This time Bluebell took off in a trot, and before I could stop her, she wheeled out of the circle of ponies and whizzed over to the ropes, where Dad and Mam were standing. I think she wanted to go home. Dad growled from far down his throat and she allowed herself to be pulled back into the circle again to join the other ponies. Too late!

The judges were calling in the winners. We were placed at the end of the line.

The lady in the headscarf spoke to each rider as she handed out rosettes. She stroked Bluebell's nose. 'That's a fine little mare you've got. What age is she?'

You could tell the way she was smiling at her that she liked the look of Bluebell.

'My Grandad thinks she might be four.'

Smiling, she handed me a purple rosette; '5th' was print-ed in gold lettering.

'Now you may do your Lap of Honour.'

I waited to see what the other riders were doing, then took off after them in a gallop around the arena. Bluebell really enjoyed this part and the spectators were clapping us. Mam and Dad looked very excited.

Afterwards Mam was patting and rubbing Bluebell like mad and Dad, asking me if I was hungry, pulled out a roll of notes. I could, I swear, have got a tenner off him.

Queueing at the chip van I looked about for Niall and Trevor.

'Hey!' A small boy was staring at Bluebell's mouth where a potato chip dangled. 'That's bold.'

I got down and yanked her head away from the bag. The boy didn't want the chip back.

In front of us in the queue, a girl turned back, the move-ment causing her golden hair to swirl about her tanned face. She was wearing jodhpurs. 'My pony does that too. Once he followed a bloke around the field trying to steal his chips. It was awful!' The chipman was passing her her chips. She had a slightly strange accent. Coming through she paused beside us. 'I'm Paula Casey.' She fed a chip to Bluebell.

'I'm Sarah Quinn.'

'I know,' she said. 'I've seen you in school.'

I remembered seeing her too. She was a new girl. Once or twice I thought I had seen her pass by our gate on a black pony.

She gave Bluebell another chip. 'Now, that's all you're getting.' She pushed her hair from her face and looked up at me. 'I go riding every day on the road and I think I know where you live. Would you like if I called for you?'

'Thanks, but I don't think I'm allowed to ride out on the road yet. Bluebell still isn't trained properly. She's very young.'

'My pony is too old. She's about a hundred.' A smile creased the corners of her wide mouth and in that instant I wished I didn't have parents who were so cautious and careful and that I could ride out the road with her because I knew it would be fun and I was sure that she would not ask me to ride with her again.

Definitely, making friends was not my strong point.

'Thanks.' I paid for my chips. They tasted good, not too greasy, and I was hungry. Paula was still standing there so I offered her one, then gave some to Bluebell.

'I see you got a prize.' Paula was looking at the rosette and I turned my pony's head so she could see it better.

'Fifth,' I answered, offering her another chip. 'Were you riding yourself?'

'No, it costs to much to enter. Four pounds, wasn't it? I have to buy my pony's feed so I don't have that much money left over. I just came for a look today when Mrs Montgomery offered me a lift. You know Mrs M? She's joint owner of the riding-school, related to Mr Boylan of the stud farm.' That was Trevor's dad.

'Not really. I don't know any horsy people.' Bluebell was nuzzling me and I gave her my last chip.

Paula put my empty chip bag and her own in a nearby rubbish bin. 'How did you get here?'

'Hacked it. It was brilliant.'

'I'll walk back with you if you like.'

'Thanks. But Dad thought Bluebell would be tired and Mr Boylan is to give us a lift in his horse-box.' Bluebell was districted, tugging and pulling at the reins and backing into people, making a nuisance of herself. 'Well, I suppose I'd better go.'

She smiled again. 'Okay, see you.'

My left foot was hardly in the stirrup when Bluebel raced off. I didn't even manage to say goodbye to Paula or tell her that I hoped to see her again, occupied as I was in keeping my balance in the saddle. Making friends was not easy.

We veered right towards the refreshments tent and Bluebell halted near a stall with boxes of fruit. Intending to get a drink I got down, loosely hooking the reins on my arm while waiting my turn. My eyes strayed to the ring where senior jumping was taking place. The figure riding his horse over the fences was Mr Boylan and when he finished there was loud clapping from some of the onlookers – Trevor and Niall to be exact. They saw me and waved, then turned their ponies around. They were coming over.

All at once angry shouts rose around me. Bluebell's head and shoulders had disappeared between the two pieces of tent canvas and this was putting the upright supporting the stall and the man with the bucket under mighty pressure. It was weird. I tugged helplessly at the reins, but she took no notice, nose and mouth rummaging at the goods on display. The delighted cackle from her was followed by the sound of creaking timber. I pulled again and gave her a smart smack with the whip. This time she responded but it only made things worse. With a quick jump to one side, she sent boxes of fruit and bars clattering on to the ground.

'Get that pony out of here!' The stall owner was clinging to the rest of his boxes. An orange had got stuck in Bluebell's teeth. Even when I pulled it from her she grinned and grinned, trying to get rid of the sour taste from her mouth, wrinkling up her lips and showing her brown teeth as if laughing at us. I pushed her out of the tent to the sound of loud squelching. A large crowd had gathered. The stall owner was breathing heavily but I think he was pleased with the new interest. 'You want a drink, okay, okay, I'll get you a drink.' He grabbed a tin of orange and made a menacing noise at Bluebell as he stuffed it into my hand. She tossed her head at him.

'Now look what you've done, spoiled that man's fruit,' I broke off, seeing Niall and Trevor leaning back in their saddles laughing. Bluebell whinnied a welcome and walked over to them.

'Hey, that was brilliant.' Niall was wiping his eyes. 'I wish my pony could do that.'

'Truly amazing,' Trevor agreed.

Bluebell was clever, I had to admit that, even as I buried my red face in her mane.

We rode off together, cantering on the grass margin of the long avenue to the Big House. We pulled in front of the grey stone building.

I said, 'Do you remember teacher telling us that this was the biggest house in Ireland?'

'Yeah, built by the richest man in Ireland,' added Trevor.

'I remember!' Niall looked at us in excitement. 'The devil appeared there at a card game. They recognised him because he had a cloven hoof where his toes should be. And when someone sprinkled holy water over him he disappeared in a puff of smoke. The marks are still there – Dad

saw them.'

Trevor reined in his pony. 'There's Dad.' A waving figure stood out from the trees.

Hayseed was first loaded into the box, Trevor walking him up the ramp. Bluebell followed and my Dad tied her securely. Then we all squeezed into the cab.

Before turning her loose in the field, I quickly removed the few remaining plaits as well as her tail bandage and hurried inside to make an important phone call.

'I got a Fifth prize. But I have to tell you, Grandad, there were only six in her competition and one was withdrawn.'

'Doesn't matter at all.' Grandad sounded in great humour. 'She wouldn't have got a prize only for she deserved it. She must have got very strong. I'll have to take a spin up to see her soon.'

It was late. I lay in bed but couldn't sleep. Called Dad and we talked on and on. Then Mam. I was tired. But one thing was keeping me awake, kept me tossing and turning. Babs was going to be in a bad mood. I wished I didn't have to go to school tomorrow. Or ever.

5 RIDING-LESSONS

The midday sun shone warmly over the slated roof of the single-storeyed school into the playground. The Infants were having a great time, some sitting on their coats by the warm school wall holding their dolls and teddies, others playing ring-a-ring-a-rosy and falling down laughing. The bigger ones were strolling around in groups. Further up the yard, Trevor and Niall were kicking football with their friends.

I was sitting alone. At break earlier I had said to Babs, 'I'm sorry about the Show, about not taking you.'

'It's okay.' Her face twisted into a smile and I knew she had it in for me.

I had taken out the rosette to show her. Flicking at the purple ribbons she said, 'It's a Fifth. Trevor got eight Firsts,' holding it loosely, almost letting it fall.

'Yeah,' Katie joined in. 'You only got a Fifth.'

Snatching it back I heard myself yelling, 'Yeah, well, Hayseed is an old pony and anyway he didn't win eight competitions. It was only eight clear rounds.'

So I was alone at lunch.

'Babs said your pony has a disease.' Grip the side of the bench with hands shaking as Katie runs off again, over to where Babs is watching, laughing. If only the bell would ring.

Then a hand fell on my shoulder and I jerked, almost falling off the bench.

'There you are. I was looking all over the yard for you.' The funny accent. Opening my eyes, I saw the thin serious face of Paula looking down at me. 'I wanted to ask how

Bluebell was after yesterday.'

'I gave her a hot bran mash last night,' I told her. 'Well, it was really just a bucket of maize. But she loved it. This morning when I was leaving, she was lying down in the field so she must have been a bit tired.'

My hands had relaxed their grip on the bench and I could feel the sun's warmth.

'Are you going to show-jump her?' Paula asked.

'I hope to. Only trouble is, I really don't know what I'm doing with her. When I'm trying to school her, she runs away with me.'

'Haven't you had any riding-lessons?'

'No. My parents don't think we need them.'

'Same here,' Paula stuck her long tanned legs out in front of her. 'My father is dead. So my Mum can't afford riding-lessons on the money she earns. I help out in Montgomery's riding-school at the weekends and in exchange will have free stabling for my pony for the winter. Hey, maybe you could get a job helping there too and get riding-lessons in exchange. Kill Show is coming up soon.'

I think it was my leg that caused the bench to slide. Paula got up to straighten it.

'That would be great,' I said. 'Thanks, Paula.'

'No problem.' She shrugged, studied her runners.

A shadow was blocking out the warmth and light of the sun and we both looked up.

'Hi, Paula.' It was Babs and Katie. A chill wind blew around the back of the school into the shelter. Babs was up to her old tricks again. Babs who took all my friends and told them lies and turned them against me. She was asking Paula to play. 'You can be on,' she offered sweetly.

'No, thanks.' Paula was frowning, turning to me, 'Do you think your parents would let you?'

She was ignoring Babs, even though Babs was still standing there. 'I'm not sure, they might! I'll ask when I get home.'

No one ever done that to Babs before.

The bell seemed to ring earlier than usual and Paula got up and hurried off to her line. Babs and Katie trailed after me saying nothing.

I'd better explain here. There were seventy-seven pupils in our year and even though Paula and I are in the same year, we were in different classrooms. This is called Random Selection.

The rest of the day flew. In the bus, across the aisle, Katie was whispering to Babs, nudging her and sniggering.

'Oh, push off!' Babs said.

When I got off, Babs was eyeing me out of the window.

In the paddock, Bluebell was lying down, her white face peering from the buttercups. Whinnying softly she unfolded her two knobbly legs and sat up on her rump. Have you ever seen a pony sitting up like a dog? They sort of look unbalanced or something, like as if their heads are too heavy for their necks. Patting her, rubbing her face against mine, remembering what the lady judge said, warm feelings rushed up inside me for this 'dark grey with the white blaze'.

'Down, Bono! Buzz off, will you? You're disturbing Bluebell,' One of her ears was folded over, the other cocked, listening. She slowly lifted on to her hind legs, staggering a little as if they were too weak to carry her. Something flickered in my stomach. 'Get up, Bluebell,' I said. Yesterday's work and excitement was too much for her. She wasn't well.

A shower of dust rose as she faltered to her feet and shook herself, head down, one ear drooping, showing no interest in anything. Bono went over and after walking around her, nosed her cheekily. A gleam showed in her blue eye. Quick turn. With a fast toss of her head, she clipped him smartly on the snout.

With a yowl, he jumped away and she took off after him,

pirouetting, jumping and bucking and diving at him while he tried to dodge the small attacking hooves. In desperation he put on a spurt, circled her, and came at her heels. With the tables turned, he barked joyously as if he had suddenly learned the rules of her game.

'Sarah, dinner!' Mam's voice rang out.

One look at Mam would tell you that she had been cleaning, even if she hadn't got the mop in her hand. Eyes red, nose twitching under one of Dad's big handkerchiefs. She is very allergic to cleaning.

Spaghetti Bolognese. Great! Between mouthfuls I told her about Paula. 'You know, the girl I met yesterday at the show.'

'I think I've seen her mother a few times down at the school. Fair-haired, tall, glamorous-looking, moved here from Australia after her husband was killed in a mining accident. He was mining superintendent someone said.' Dabbing at her eyes. 'She lives near Mooneen Cross. Don't you know that old house covered in ivy? His parents were supposed to have left it to her. She's an architect of some sort. Can't have much business in these times.' She was smiling. 'Well, I'm glad you've made friends with Paula. That's her name, isn't it?'

'Yeah. She works at the riding-school on Saturdays. She's going to ask Mrs Montgomery if I can help there in return for riding-lessons. Please, Mam, could I? Bluebell badly needs a few lessons and so do I. You saw the way she raced away at the Show. When she decides to go, I have no control. Nothing.'

'Bluebell certainly does need to know who is in charge.' She got up. 'I'd better finish the floor. You start your homework right away.'

'But Mam . . . about my riding-lessons?'

'We've been considering getting you a lesson. Maybe you could follow it up, this idea of Paula's – they are expensive, you know. See what Dad says when he gets home.'

My geography book was just out on the table when hoof-beats sounded outside and Paula rode past the kitchen window. With the sudden opening of the door, she dropped her whip in surprise. I picked it up and handed it to her.

'Thanks,' she smiled. 'I just wanted to find out if you were going down to the riding-school next Saturday. Did you ask your mum? What did she say?'

'She's going to ring Mrs Montgomery about a lesson as soon as Dad gets home.' My leg was hopping.

'You mean she's going to pay for a lesson for you! Lucky you.' She fixed a strand of her pony's hair. 'If you're going down on Saturday, try and make it for around three o'clock and I can call for you and we could go down together.'

'Thanks.' I had already noticed that she doesn't get excited much about things like me and Babs. She's kind of calm, sophisticated. Like a movie star.

You could tell her pony was old by the white hairs breaking through his black ones. He stood quietly with his head hanging, taking no notice of me patting him.

'Ouch!'

'Blackie! Don't do that!' Paula chucked his reins. 'Sorry, did he hurt you?' looking anxiously at the tooth mark on my hand.

'It didn't hurt,' I lied, embarrassed at my stupidity. A real horsy person like her wouldn't let that happen.

She brought him round again. 'His previous owners let him do what he liked, so he's picked up a few bad habits. But he's still a very good pony.' She yanked his head from the flower basket.

'Can he jump?' Tugging Mam's prize aubrietia out of his mouth.

'Yeah. he's a very good jumper when he wants to. But he has laminitis and goes lame sometimes.'

'How does it affect him?'

'His feet get so sore he can't walk on them. For him it's like walking on fire. Ponies get it by being left out on good grass and getting too fat.'

No fear Bluebell was going to have that problem. She had been on good grass for ages now and was still skinny.

Blackie was nibbling at the fresh growth of the rose-trees. 'I'll have to go,' she wheeled him about. 'Still have to do some mucking out and we've got a lot of homework. And I have to cook the dinner this evening because Mum will be late home and she's always so tired.'

Mam still hadn't contacted Mrs M about the riding-lessons and I had no news for Paula when she came to join me on the bench at playtime. Babs had been exploding milk cartons with the boys and throwing them in the bin and she raced across to us, mouth turned right down at the corners.

'Me and Katie are fighting,' voice small and injured, like water going down a plughole, her cardigan trailing in the dust. 'I don't like her any more. She let my puppy fall.'

Paula's long eyebrows wiggled in a straight line.

I said, 'You haven't got a puppy.' It was true. This was just Babs' way of getting sympathy. 'You told me Finn now had no puppies, that your dad had them put to sleep.'

She twisted the sleeve of her cardigan. 'Well, we have one left. And Dad didn't put the others to sleep. The pet rabbit ate them. This was the littlest puppy of them all. Katie was cruel to him.'

This new tactic of Babs was worrying and I gave a quick look at Paula. Rustle of paper. Babs was taking out a chocolate bar, a peppermint bar. My favourite. She took off the paper, and my mouth watered. 'Have a piece.' Offering it to Paula. 'Here, have another square,' again inviting her.

'Thanks.' Paula took it, put it in her mouth and got up off the bench. 'Want to walk around?' she said to me.

'What about your friends?' I asked. She never seemed to be on her own.

'They're not interested in ponies. By the way, I've got some old pony magazines that Mrs M gave me, if you'd like to borrow them. They've got useful tips.'

Babs butted in. 'My dad says he's going to get me a pony too. An Arab pony. He's going to Arabia on business next week and he's getting me one. From a Sheik.'

'Blackie is part Arab,' Paula said. 'We couldn't afford a pure-bred Arab. Lucky you.' She said it as if she didn't care, in a bored sort of way.

Babs wouldn't give up. 'Katie isn't my friend any more.'

Then we saw her. Now Katie, I thought, you know what it's like to sit on the bench with no one to play with and feel miserable. It serves you right.

Going home on the bus, Babs moved up to sit beside me, ignoring Katie. When I got off, Katie got off too. Her face was all squashed.

'Could I see your pony?'

I opened the gate and she came in.

After she'd gone I ran into the house. 'It's all arranged!' Mam was chopping up cabbage leaves for Bono's dinner. 'You have a lesson tomorrow at three o'clock in the indoor riding-school. It will be a joint lesson with one other pupil and Mrs Montgomery herself will instruct. She sounded very nice.'

I rang Paula straight away. She didn't get very excited or anything but I could tell she was pleased. 'Mrs M is the best teacher down there, but a bit lah di dah. It's better when there are no more than two, but a group lesson is cheaper. I had a group lesson once on Blackie in the indoor arena.'

'How did you get on?'

'He wouldn't jump at all. It was awful.' She giggled.

And how would Bluebell do, I wondered as I put down the phone. That evening, she got more schooling than usual.

'Are you sure you'll be safe riding down the road on your own.' As usual, Mam was worrying.

'Don't worry, we'll be fine. I've read the rules of the road. As well as that, Paula has ridden up and down from the riding-school loads of times and she has done her Riding and Road Safety Test, didn't you, Paula?'

Paula, looked down her nose at Blackie's flank, calmly moving him out of the way as he tried to nip Bluebell. "There's no problem.'

After half an hour's riding in the field, the ponies were more at ease with each other. Then we moved off. Out on the road, we travelled in single file, Blackie in the lead as he was the most experienced and we kept well in on the left.

A tractor came around the corner and Paula pulled in on the verge in front to let it pass. Bluebell dismissed it as 'kids' stuff'. Further down, past Manning's, just before the Y junction, a big truck rounded the bend and came towards us. There was no room for us to pass. I pulled Bluebell up and prepared to turn and go back up the hill to an entrance. Steady, Bluebell. There was no turning back. because a car had crept right up behind us. Boxed in, Bluebell started shaking, showing the whites of her eyes. There was nowhere we could go. Easy, Bluebell. We're going to get sandwiched. But what was Paula doing? Space was narrowing, ditch too steep to climb on. She had her hand in the air. Like a lollipop lady she signalled the truck driver to stop and he pulled up, allowing us to pass.

At the junction, all was quiet with no traffic in sight. Paula told me to stay on my own side and she crossed into the middle, indicating she was turning right with an outstretched hand. We got across safely. The covered riding-school glistened through the trees. I was glad to turn off the road and up the pot-holed avenue.

'Next time, she'll be better,' Paula told me 'She wasn't bad at all for a novice.'

Paula led the way to the door of the indoor arena. From inside the sheet iron came the soft thud of hooves and a women's high and shrill voice giving instructions. Paula leaned over as the door opened inwards. 'You'd better go in,' she hissed.

But Bluebell for some reason wouldn't budge, even when Paula got off her pony and took the bridle. A man came riding out on a tall brown horse and clattered away.

'Paula, how are you?' A tiny woman appeared in the doorway, wearing jodhpurs and a pink anorak. 'And is this the little mare?' She came over to us, walking with a kind of hobble, as if her legs had been broken over the years, in a thousand places and fixed in a kind of curve.

'It's Mrs M,' Paula mouthed silently behind her back.

'And you must be Sarah. I was speaking to your mother on the 'phone. You've done some riding before, haven't you? Good. The other girl hasn't arrived yet. She's late.'

She took hold of Bluebell's bridle, saying 'All right, little girl,' in a firm, quiet voice. She led her into the arena.

'Just warm her up, walk her around, to get her used to her new surroundings. Then you can show us what you can do.' Paula waited at the door for me to pass. 'I have to go and help the little ones tack up. See you after.'

It felt strange in here. We were all alone. There was a very big echo and gusts of high wind and rain rattled the sheet iron, making Bluebell tense. She was putting up her head and pulling on the bit, rushing about, and every time she passed the big door it clattered noisily and she swerved towards it, wanting to get out and go home. My arms were already stiff from holding her. I kept remembering that I should be talking to her, but it is not easy having a conversation with your pony when she's not listening. Besides I was tense myself.

'This way,' Mrs M's voice echoed around the arena. 'Now, take her around the other way. Anti-clockwise. Remember things look different when you approach from the other side. Good. Change directions. Walk again.'

Bluebell whinnied anxiously, looking for Blackie.

The door gusted open. Outside I could see a girl and a

pony. A woman beside her clutched a saddle. In the sand arena beyond, the tots' lesson was taking place. Paula was holding a tiny Shetland pony while the rider mounted, helping to put her feet in the stirrups.

Mrs M hobbled across to the door. 'You did say your daughter Claire could ride.' She sounded impatient.

'Yes, but we were unable to secure the saddle this morning. We couldn't tie the girth.'

'Take that off,' ordered Mrs M, 'You won't need it in here.' The girl took off her full-length waxed coat, to reveal the mauve-coloured suede chaps that protected her white jodhpurs. Across her sweater was written "Patella Dressage Society'. 'Now, bring your pony in. Be firm.'

Claire pulled and tugged at the reins but the pony's head was up, feet pressed stubbornly in the ground.

Mrs M went behind with the whip. 'Go on!'

The pony bulldozed through without warning, almost trampling down the woman and bruising the girl against the door. I rode Bluebell to the other end, out of harm's way.

'Are you all right, Claire?' Mrs M's voice was loud, in control. The girl nodded, trying to keep a grip on her prancing pony. Mrs M spoke sharply to him and he seemed to quieten down. She lifted on the saddle of polished leather and tied the girth without delay and then showed Claire how to adjust the leathers. After giving her a leg up, she checked and tightened the girth again, explaining that it often needed further tightening because a pony can puff himself out. Lastly, she handed her the whip. 'Keep it in your right hand for the moment. Now, walk him on. On the right rein, clockwise.'

I wondered if I could ever be as well turned out as that girl and her pony. A beautiful cream colour, it had a flowing mane and small dish face. But right now his ears were back and his eyes were rolling wickedly. He was stepping high, ready to go. I decided I'd invest the fiver I got from

Babs' father in a hoof-pick, the start of a big self improvement job – for Bluebell.

Mrs M told the girl to walk him slowly, to soothe him and he'd settle down. 'Yes, he's a bit nappy, isn't he?'

The mother was anxiously twisting the lead rope in her hands. 'We haven't got him long. He's a little too fast for her. The other pony was too slow.'

'Whoa . . a!'

The pony had broken past Bluebell and was rushing in a small tight circle, the girl clinging to the mane.

'Calm him!' shouted Mrs M.

'I can't,' she wailed.

'Talk to him. Sit deep in your saddle and don't swing out of him.'

Suddenly the pony stopped and reared but the girl stayed on. Mrs M marched over. 'Push him on with your legs. Give me that whip! What's this? Using spurs on that pony! Take them off.'

'Sarah,' Mrs M instructed me, 'Ride Bluebell in front. Give him a lead. Now, on the left rein.'

Claire was too busy clinging to the bridge of her saddle to even glance at me. I trotted in front and her pony followed.

The mother's voice carried faintly across the arena, 'When we were buying him, the owner told us, "Look what a great pony he is. Just sit up on him and ride him around the yard." We didn't realise he had so many bad habits. We're hoping that by stabling him here with you, his manners might improve.'

Mrs M sounded angry. 'That pony is not suitable for a beginner.'

Bluebell was moving quite well now and the other pony seemed calmer, although Claire was still clinging to the saddle.

Mrs M shouted to her, 'If you think your pony is going to bolt, don't panic. He can't get too far here. Now, instead of standing up and leaning forward, sit well down on your behind. That's what it's for. It's not an ornament!'

Claire muttered in a cranky voice, 'I know that.' But she stayed crouched.

It was valuable advice for me too, and when Bluebell tried to break from a trot into a canter, I was able to check her.

Mrs M called us into the centre of the ring. 'You both have young ponies, very different in temperament I might say, and you both want them to bring them to Kill Show.'

Mam must have been telling her!

'The first and most basic thing a rider must learn is to sit properly on her horse. Then to get your pony to do exactly what you ask him to do. How to go forward. How to stop. How to bend right and left . . . Now, Claire, don't chuck your pony in the mouth. You're hurting him, he's confused and he's not going to respond when he doesn't understand what you want him to do. Keep a light but steady contact.'

In a voice that would have filled the Point Depot, Mrs M

boomed out instructions. Start! Stop! Turn! Bluebell managed all of it correctly. But the cream pony was 'uneven'. Mrs M led us to some painted barrels. In turn, we walked between them, bending in and out as she directed. Again Bluebell learned quickly whereas the other pony tried to take some short-cuts.

Mrs M placed a large potato on the ground. 'Now, ride to the other end of the arena, come back, pick up that potato and bring it to me.' Bluebell stood quietly when I got down to pick up the potato and got back up. When Claire got down, her pony broke free and cantered off. Mrs M had to hold him for her. 'Now trr . . . rot!'

Eventually Mrs M called us back into the centre. 'Well done. It's not just your ponies that have had to work hard today. Dismount and give them a big pat.'

We both got down. I fed Bluebell some porridge oatlets from my pocket. Claire's mother passed her a tissue to wipe her eyes.

Mrs M cleared her throat. 'For the next day, I want you to study your pony manuals. You've both got one, have you? If not, borrow one. I want you to be able to describe your pony, giving each part its proper name and to know the different parts of your tack and your grooming kit.'

Our first lesson was over. And maybe my last, unless Paula had got me the job. I met her with the Shetland pony and rider in hand.

'How did it go?'

'Great. Bluebell was terrific.'

'You can put her in here,' she held a stable door open for me. 'And then you'd better help me to muck out.'

'You mean, I've got the job?'

'You have a job here every Saturday, in return for which you'll get half an hour's riding-lesson per week.'

'I don't believe it!' I slid down off Bluebell. 'When, when can I start?'

'Next Saturday. Now put your pony in there and grab

that shovel. We've ten stables to do.'

As we mucked out together I described to Paula every single thing that happened during the lesson. 'Yeah, I did that too,' handing me the fork to remove the heap of dung from the sawdusted floor, working on the loose stuff herself with the shovel. Then she was back after emptying the wheelbarrow, resting it at the doorway. 'Don't look now, but isn't that your friend Trevor over there?'

Mr Boylan and Trevor were tacking up a pony. 'He must be going in for the advanced jumping lesson.' Paula glanced at her watch. 'He's in your class, isn't he? Aren't you going to talk to him?'

'Yeah, well, I don't really want to.' Funny! I would have gone straight over if Niall had been with him. But Trevor was different. After every few forkfuls, I looked over to see if he had noticed me, in the hope of catching his eye. Ready to smile and wait for him to come strolling over. Fat chance! He swung into the saddle and went towards the arena.

Shouts and the skittering of hooves on concrete pavement on my right. Paula and I hurried over to help. The cream-coloured pony was refusing to go into the stall prepared for him, lashing out in all directions.

Mr Boylan came over. He and Mrs M slung a lunge rein above the pony's hocks and forced him in. For a while the door vibrated from his kicks.

'The rogue,' Trevor's father muttered to Mrs M. 'I'd get rid of him. Dangerous animal.' He turned and saw me. 'Well, Sarah. Down for a lesson? That pony of yours is the right type. Bomb proof.'

'Thanks, Mr Boylan.' I walked back past the white face peering over the half door. When we were finished and I led Bluebell out to join Paula, Trevor had disappeared.

On the way home, Paula said I could borrow her pony manual for the lessons.

6 JUMPING

Grass spurts green and glossy in fields overhung by wide ditches where the colourful hawthorn caps and spills out over boreens and motorways. Small oak and beech-trees mingling along the fringes of the old wood show young green, and in the gardens fresh wet clay sprouts and gurgles.

The next few weeks went flying by. I had little time for anything after school other than riding in the field and organising myself for the Saturday job. But I had to fit homework and music lessons somewhere in between.

Helping with the tiny tots was fun. I'd put on their bridles, give them a whoosh up and run alongside as they trotted. They were for ever slipping off, as their legs were so short. They didn't even cry after a fall (except when the mothers were looking on). Then you just whooshed them back up.

Paula arrived on Blackie most evenings and, with me as the riding instructress, we had 'debriefing' sessions. (The 'debriefing' was Paula's phrase – she'd heard it in a spy movie.) Paula was already very knowledgeable from her work at the school. For instance she knew that a pony has a hoof not a foot, and, theoretically, how to tell a pony's age by its teeth, although that was still a tricky one. But there were other things she wasn't too sure of, such as the various parts of the pony and how to describe a pony, Bluebell being 'an iron-grey, one wall eye, three white socks, a white blaze between the eyes, a whorl on her left flank.' A whorl is like a fingerprint – no two are the same.

We put our ponies through all the flatwork exercises Mrs

M had taught me, turning and twisting them around buckets and old bits of beds and anything else that we had rescued from hedges and ditches. Blackie seemed to have done it all before. To improve our own seat and balance, we rode without stirrups and without saddles (tough on the leg muscles), 'scissoring' about, that is, the rider doing a full turn around on the pony's back. This was all good fun. But the jumping-lesson, my last lesson, was the most exciting. In preparation, Bluebell had walked and trotted over poles on the ground and had got quite knacky and I was able to steer her much better.

'Elbows in, heels down, toes in – you're not doing ballet dancing now. Sit straight as if your belly button was tied with elastic to the mane. If you look where you're going, you'll go where you're looking. Don't look down at your pony! She's still underneath you. You'll know soon enough if she isn't.'

The jumps were about half-barrel height. Mrs M stood in the centre of the arena, legs apart, hands on hips.

'Trot on. You're going to canter in the next corner. Prepare her, sitting up, shoulders back. Inside leg on the girth, outside leg behind the girth. Ask now! Yes! Don't let her break, keep your legs on her all the time. Okay. Slow her to a trot in this corner. Easy! Whoa! Steady the trot before coming back to walk. Now, next time, I want you to do exactly as you did there, only this time don't come back to trot. Just head straight for these fences here. Off you go!'

I squeezed with my legs and Bluebell moved off slowly.

'Wake her up. Use your legs! Squeeze. That's it!'

My legs made loud slapping noises, pushing and pushing her into canter.

'Circle her into the jump.' A single fence, yellow and black, with a pole in front to help to judge the take-off point.

'She's going to stop! Push her on. Hunt her over it,' Mrs M was yelling.

There was a rush of air and we landed.

'That's it! Good! Now the next one. Get her to move!'

The next fence was a spread of two poles. I leaned forward and Bluebell went up and over.

'Much better. Well done!' Mrs M spoke in ordinary tones again. 'Slow down. Pat her. Talk to her. That's good. Now, I'm going to ask you to do that once more.'

This time we had two extra fences to jump, a cross pole and a parallel.

I was beginning to feel more confident now. Up there in the saddle, I'm pushing Bluebell into the jumps, legs smacking, bottom pushing down, holding a conversation with her. It's okay, Bluebell. You can do it. We'll make it. And there's Bluebell thundering along, going up and over. I think that no obstacle is too great for her, but Mrs M says we've to keep the fences low, not to face her with anything too high, in that way building up her confidence. We canter along together over the jumps, deaf to everything only Mrs M's instructions, taking the jumps one after the other.

'Good! That's enough for one day.' Mrs M patted Bluebell warmly. 'You'll have a lot of fun on that little pony. She is very honest and willing, just needs more schooling.'

'Orange juice, Paula?'

'Thanks.'

I elbowed the fridge shut and carried out the glasses. Paula was holding the big plate under Bluebell's muzzle. She quietly ate her way through a feed of porridge and apple skins. Whistling sounds of pleasure came from her as she munched off Mam's patterned Carrigaline pottery, her big head in the doorway. There was no prize for manners. She licked the plate and swept the spillages off the floor, accepting the slice of tart offered to her.

'I'd like to join the Pony Club.' Paula was frowning hard. 'But I hate asking Mum for more money. We still have to

pay the blacksmith to do Blackie's set of shoes. Then there's
Kill Show.'

'Can't you get it somewhere?'

Sometimes Dad and Mam said they had no money but
they always seemed to be able to come up with it. But I felt
that somehow it was not the same for Paula. The thought
that she couldn't join with me gave me a fluttery feeling in
my stomach.

'I could maybe save up something out of my pocket-
money.' She put away the brush. 'I have to go now.'

Dad was late home and came up to my bedroom to say
goodnight.

'It is true, Dad, what Mrs M said about Bluebell, that she
is an honest pony. When she had eaten her oatlets and
smelled more in my pocket, she looked at me as if to say
"No, that's not mine." '

Dad smiled in the dim light. 'What Mrs Montgomery
meant is that she is willing and anxious to do what is asked
of her. In other words, she's a trier.'

'She's that surely. I know she'll jump the fences at Kill
Show. I just know she will . . . Dad, do you think Paula and
me will be able to go?'

'Paula and I,' he corrected. 'We'll have to wait and see if
we can find transport. Now, say your prayers.'

I prayed that we'd find a horse-box somewhere. But first
of all we had work to do.

In the porch, Paula carefully removed her riding-boots.
'They're muddy,' apologising to Mam. 'I was mucking out
so I probably smell of horse. Hope you're not allergic to
horse dust, Mrs Quinn.

'Just house dust, Paula.' Mam was sipping her coffee.
'You seem to be a very hardworking girl. How do you manage to do school homework?'

Paula sounded very grown-up. 'I can do it in the morning. I'm an early riser.'

Mam is very impressed by good manners and sense and hard work and stuff like that. I could see she liked Paula.

'Come on,' I said, 'we'd better get started.' This was our project jumping course!

Outside, we did a scan of the hedges and boundaries of the fields and paddock, 'I knew they were here somewhere.' We rolled out the two tar barrels into the middle of the field. Wiping our hands free of rust, we collected the red and white paint Dad had left for us in the tool-shed and the old paintbrushes left soaking in a dirty oil tin.

Paula uncovered several long timber poles hidden in the hedge. They were heavy and awkward, but we managed to free them from the ivy and we carried one over to the tar barrels.

'Good,' Paula nodded. 'I'll set it out for painting.' On the pole, she marked the divisions for the paint stripes. 'Be careful with the paint,' she warned. 'Wipe it on the side of the tin or it will drip. Here, I'll show you. Mum let me

paint our garden gate last Saturday.' Completing a few strokes, she handed it back, picked up the stirring stick. 'Stir paint from the bottom.'

We painted the barrels, then the pole. The evening was bright and warm.

'Hi!' A loud jangle and Bab's voice drifted down off the top of the ditch. I shaded my eyes against the sun.

'We're making jumps for Bluebell and Blackie.' Paula kept brushing away, damp beads on her forehead.

Babs stared at her gloomily. Nobody spoke. After watching for a while, she went off.

The sun was getting warmer. Paula wiped her forehead, paintbrush still in hand. 'I've nearly finished this part.'

The paint dripped on the ground and on to my shoes. My hands were plastered with red.

'It's ready now, I think.' Paula put down her brush on the tin lid.

I wiped my hands on the old rag. 'It's a super jump.'

'Yeah, it's good all right.'

Then I told her about the furze – Dad had stacked the cuttings of furze bushes for burning. She was enthusiastic. 'We could make a brush fence from them. Ponies love natural fences.'

Dick came over from his potato patch to help us. He punched lots of holes in the sod with a crowbar and we stuffed the bush cuttings into these holes, getting our hands scratched and full of thorns. Then he directed us to a stack of old tyres. We propped a pole on two small water barrels, lacing the tyres through it. There was an old tree log over near the swing, and he gave us a hand rolling it over. Our course was finished!

'Perfect,' breathed Paula. I had to agree. We now had four interesting fences, making up a proper jumping course, like they have in riding-schools.

After Dick had poured oil on our hands, we wiped them on the old rag and dock leaves. 'I'd better get Blackie.'

Paula cycled off so fast that she skidded around the turn.

And I hurried away to get Bluebell's saddle, all tiredness gone now that it was time for action.

Mrs M's instructions were clear in my head: 'First you get your pony to walk, then trot, over ground poles, just to warm up and get their pacing in order.'

Bluebell did this part very nicely. The brush fence was next. She trotted up to it and cleared it, taking such a huge jump that she almost flung me out over her head. She grazed and watched as I adjusted the painted pole on the two barrels, keeping them from rolling with horse dung.

'That pole might be too high for her.' Leaning on his spade, Dick was shaking his head solemnly.

'Bluebell is well able. Watch!'

Slowly trotting into it, she stuck her head over it and refused to go any further. The next time I really rode her on, using my legs and feet. Going over the jump I leaned forward, letting her neck stretch out. Great!

'Hi.' Paula pushed open the gate, leaning over Blackie's neck.

It was clear that her pony was well used to fences. After warming up, she galloped him straight for the jumps and he went up and over. Only trouble was, coming into a jump he had a trick of slowing down, as if he were about to refuse, and then he'd hop over.

'What's all this?' Dad joined us in the field, looking rumpled, tie loosely knotted.

'Just watch, Dad.'

This time, Bluebell cleared the jumps at a canter.

'Now, it's your turn, Paula.' I steered Bluebell into the jumps after Blackie.

'Well done!' Dad went around and examined the fences. 'Fast work, you're two fine course builders.' He got down on his hunkers to examine the bush fence. 'You got a bit of help on this one, Dick?' glancing up smiling at us.

'Yeah, well, we told him what to do,' I said.

He straightened up. 'And your ponies are going well?' patting their sweating sides as they heaved in and out under us. He paused. 'Better not to overdo it, though,' looking at Bluebell.

'Bluebell isn't tired. She loves it.' I wheeled her about for another round and Paula did the same.

But Dad's hand stayed, resting lightly on the reins. 'Remember what Grandad said. Ten minutes of jumping a day is enough for a young pony. It's different with an experienced pony.' He glanced at Blackie.

Paula was patting her pony hard. 'Yeah, well, Blackie has done a lot of jumping.'

Dad went on, 'Now, Bluebell is different.' As soon as he started again about the importance of walking and trotting, clockwise and anti-clockwise, to build up muscle, make her supple, I got a fit of yawning and Paula was fidgeting at her reins.

'We'll do that tomorrow, Dad.'

'I have to go anyway,' Paula swung her pony around towards the gate. 'I'll be down again tomorrow,' she called back.

After tea, I led Bluebell to the side of the house where Dad wanted to measure her. The uncomfortable fluttery was back feeling in my stomach, like a seasicknes or something. Must be all the paint. Bluebell has grown, I'm sure. It was not quite as easy to vault up on her as before. And when he lined her up with the wall and marked her shoulder height using a level, he nodded in agreement. 'She's 120 cms. She has grown all right. Maybe it's her nature to be thin.'

'Measure me, Dad.'

Bluebell watched through the open door. Part of our kitchen wall hasn't been painted since I was three years old. That's where Dad has inked a record of my height over the years. He studied the measuring tape and laughed. 'You and Bluebell are growing at the same rate.'

'I don't want to be too big for her.' The uncomfortable feeling had not faded completely.

'Not to worry. You can get a bigger pony later on, if you do outgrow her.' Dad threw his tape into the press.

Again that feeling. 'I'll never part with Bluebell.'

'Hi, Paula.' Babs was real friendly. 'Want to play with us?'

Paula had been with some of her classmates. When she saw me she started over but Babs and Katie got there first.

'No, thanks.' Paula eyed Katie, aloof, cool. She continued past them to me. 'We're just hanging around. Want to join us?' There was a warm smile on her serious face.

Her friends were staring at me curiously. 'Please, I want you to.' I followed her over.

'Who asked you to join?'

'I did, Fanny.' Paula's quiet voice cut through the din of the playground. She wedged me in beside her in the group and we strolled around. A girl called Maeve was talking about a disco and what she would wear. On the far side, Fanny kept glaring at me. It was a bit off-putting. My eyes kept straying to the bench. Babs and Katie had gone over to sit there.

Paula turned to me. 'There's a Starter Stakes competition for beginners at Kill Show – it's called Clear Round Jumping. If you and I practise enough, we might be ready to enter for it.'

My leg gave a mighty jerk. 'Niall and Trevor usually go in that competition.' I tried to sound cool. 'And they do pretty well. It would be terrific if we could go too.'

'If only we had some way of getting our ponies there . . .'

If only every day could be like this! Paula and I strolling around the yard together discussing our plans for the next show, just the two of us, seeing as Fanny and the others find pony talk boring.

7 SHOW FEVER

The sun shining high in the sky warmed the hill and lit up the wide valley in its silky green. In the garden, delphiniums mixed colours with lupins and roses and the purple flowers of the Golden Wonders over in the potato patch. Swallows flew in to their nests in the garage.

As the Show drew nearer, my confidence in Bluebell grew.

Paula and I had stopped worrying about how we were going to get our ponies there. We were working hard at training them.

The ground being hard from lack of rain, I went easy on the jumping in case Bluebell's feet got sore. But Paula! I'd never before seen her this determined. She put Blackie over the jumps a thousand times. The only trouble was, he was a little unpredictable. Sometimes he flew over the fence. Other times he came galloping straight on, head down, full tilt, so that she couldn't control him, then – at the last minute – swerving sideways, he would jolt her out of the saddle and up on to his neck. And when she tapped him with the whip to correct him, his head dropped even further. Then sometimes he would stop suddenly and Paula would sail over the jump, alone. Luckily she's a really good rider and most times she managed to stay on. But he was difficult. As for the figure eight he wasn't into maths at all.

Bluebell was different. She went calmly for her jumps. And you should see the style and grace of her, turning and twisting in answer to the reins, pivoting on her tiny hooves.

After finishing schooling, we would race our ponies up and down the field and that was the best fun of all.

Galloping, pulling away from each other, shouting and screaming to the thunder of hooves.

One day Paula and I were at the school door when Niall pulled in on his bicycle.

'So you're ready for the Show?' he said. 'I'd like to go too. We had good fun last time.'

'If you go,' I said gloomily, 'you'll probably see me falling off . . . I might need to get Bluebell shod. Will you tell your dad to call?'

'Sure.' He opened the door for me, making a low bow, and I noticed his dodgy new haircut as the Principal swept past.

'Thank you, Niall. The age of chivalry isn't dead yet!'

'You just killed it, a Mhaistreas.' Redfaced and grinning, he let the door swing in my face.

'Well, thanks.' I pretended to examine my nose.

He can be such a goof sometimes.

Dad came in from work and went straight to his study, sitting on the armchair with eyes closed, hands resting on his arms. The deep ridge on his forehead had a 'please don't disturb' written all over it.

But I couldn't wait. 'Well, Dad?'

Eyes opened slowly. 'Eh?'

'The box, Dad,' I prompted.

'The box? Oh, you mean the oats? It's in the porch.'

'Thanks, Dad. I was talking about the horse-box. Did you get it?'

'Oh, the horse-box. No, the one I was promised is a ton weight or more. It's far too heavy for my car.'

'But, Dad,' arrest those closing eyes, 'The Show is on in two days' time!'

'I know. I'm sorry, Sarah. It doesn't look as if we can get you there.'

'We could hack it, like last time.'

'Sarah, it's more than sixteen miles there and back.' He

picked up a newspaper.

'Oh, Dad. You promised!'

He looked up sharply. 'I promised to do my best to get it and I did that.' The paper rattled ferociously. 'Will you answer the door?'

Mam got there first. Paula was smiling politely at her, hands on the bars of her bike. 'Is Sarah there? Thanks, Mrs Quinn, but I can't stay. I'm supposed to be getting the tea.' She raised her eyebrows questioningly at me as Mam went in and I closed the door behind us.

'Oh!' The disappointed way she said it made me feel worse about the horse-box. We walked slowly down the driveway together, Paula pushing her bike, elbows leaning on it, head downcast.

'I was hoping Mum could borrow Betty's box — that's her friend,' she explained. 'Betty is very horsey. She blows hot and cold, even though Mum looks after her Rottweiler when she's away. She promised us the box last time but it didn't work out, so there's no point counting on her.'

I threw a stick for Bono. 'What about Mrs M? She has a box, hasn't she?'

Paula looked at me thoughtfully, dark threads in her blue eyes. 'She's probably taking some ponies to the Show, but we could ask her.'

I raced back to get my bike. We were away before anyone could ask us where we were going.

Bursting in through the back door, out of breath. 'Mam, Dad! Mrs M said we could have her box because she won't be using it. We'll be able to go after all.'

Mam put down the newspaper and Dad paused at the sink, suds dropping from his hands.

'Free of charge,' Paula suddenly grabbed me. I'd never seen her like this before. She was giggling madly and we jumped up and down, hugging and laughing.

Mam said, 'I hope you're not imposing on people.'

Paula stopped. 'Oh, no. She told us, "You can have the double box, it's light and I won't be using it. The two ponies will fit nicely." '

Our worries about getting to the Show were over!

'Mum will tow it over on Sunday morning. We can load the ponies there.' She suddenly checked her watch. 'I forgot, I promised Mum I'd be home.' The serious look was back on her face as she hurried for the door.

Dad was having his tea. 'Good to see you doing things for yourselves.' He sounded in better form.

Still there is only so much you can do by yourself. Something was bothering me. Tomorrow was the day before the Show. No point in asking Babs or Katie to help me to get Bluebell ready. I'd have to do it on my own this time.

The gate clanged and Bono took off down the slope barking wildly. It was Niall's dad. I hurried down to catch Bluebell. It was important that she got shod this time, because there was some rule about a four-year-old needing two front shoes.

'Easy, now, easy.' Willie lifted her front leg. 'Be the hokey, her hooves are like timber. Big and strong.' Reaching into the boot of his car he took out two small shoes and measured them against her hooves. Not one inch too big! Bluebell stood quietly while he pared her front hooves, but after a while she grew tired and tried to put down the leg Willie was working on. 'Easy, easy, pet,' Willie's voice was soothing, working away with his rasp and hammer. The bag of grass I had pulled for her was empty.

When he had gone, I left Bluebell grazing on the grass. Mam met me at the door and kissed me. 'Bluebell will be the star of the show.'

I wished I could believe her.

I was up early, hurrying out to the paddock where the dew

still clung in shiny wet drops to the grass. I loosened Bluebell's tail bandage and watched her tail fall in silver and yellow waves down to her hocks. It looked well. But her mane was still the same, bristling on the ridge of her neck like a brush. Mam was calling me for breakfast.

But first Bluebell was given her bucket of oats. Grandad had told me that she would need it to put some fizz into her.

Inside Dad was knocking back a huge slice of brown bread, thick lump of cheddar cheese on top. All I could manage was a slice of toast.

I pulled up my jodhpurs and heard the loud sound of a rip. There it was on the inside of the leg.

'Give it to me.' Mam stitched quickly.

'Where's my white shirt? Who took my hat? I'm supposed to be down at Paula's at half-past nine.'

Dad was putting on his jacket and offered to walk with us. 'Bluebell might be a little frisky after the oats.'

'She won't, Dad.' How would Bluebell know she was going to a show?

But no sooner had Dad let us out through the gate than she started acting up, shying and prancing and breaking into a canter. By the time we reached Paula's house, my arms were pulled out of their sockets. Bluebell made straight for the paddock at the back, whinnying loudly, where Blackie was receiving the attention of Paula and her brothers. They clustered around him, thumping and rubbing him with cloths. His mane and tail were neatly plaited and his hind quarters had a rich shine. I don't know why it was but I found it hard to smile at Paula. Not that she was too happy looking herself. She tossed her rubber to Dan and came over to join me.

'Hi.' Rolling her eyes towards the tall guy who was stomping about in long hunting boots. Adrian, her eldest brother, went to boarding school and came home for weekends. She had already told me about him.

'Blackie looks great,' I said.

'So does Bluebell. Her tail is super.'

'Not that way! This way!' With a sudden bellow Adrian grabbed a cloth from little Dan, gave a quick demonstration and handed it back. Thumbs tucked inside the belt of his jodhpurs, he stood with legs wide apart. 'Come on! That isn't good enough. More elbow grease.' Dan was growing red and looked as if he was going to cry. Adrian came strolling up to us, taking big long steps. I was trying to stop giggling and so was Paula.

'Blackie is going nicely. I have him pretty well schooled now.' His eyes flickered over Bluebell. 'That yours? Oh well.' He shrugged. He might as well have finished, 'She's not in the running!' I could see what Paula meant about him. What a pain!

'I would probably win the jumping competition,' he went on. 'Paula doesn't know how to manage Blackie. She lets him do whatever he likes. She's not strong enough for him.' He swaggered over to Blackie again.

Paula made a face behind his back. 'Mum says I have to share Blackie with him today. He thinks he's great. He makes me do all the training and the mucking out all week and then he just comes along and sits up.'

Wheels sounded on the gravel. We were so excited to see the horse-box that we gave a big cheer. Mrs Casey got out of the car and slipped off her tinted glasses to have a better look at Bluebell. 'Does she travel well?' nervously tapping the lobe of the glasses against gleaming white teeth. Her face was oval-shaped like Paula's.

'I think so.'

She called out, 'Adrian, lead Blackie up first,' and ignored Paula beside her.

But Bluebell refused to follow Blackie into the box. Then Blackie started fretting on his own, tossing his head and pushing against the partition and messing.

'Put some nuts into the bucket,' Mrs Casey ordered

Paula, and taking Bluebell by the lead rope herself, she walked her up, holding the bucket in front.

At the showgrounds, the ponies unloaded easily and leaving Dan and Adrian to hold them we went straight over to the caravan marked 'Entries' with our money.

'Name?' the girl at the window looked up.

I told her and said I was the owner of Bluebell Mountain.

'What do you want to enter?'

'Clear Round Jumping.' She took my money and gave me a white card with the number 168 on a string to tie around my waist.

Paula gave her name as the owner of 'Woollongong Lad' — that was Blackie's show name. The woman said 'Clear Round Jumping is taking place in Pony Ring 2,' pointing with her pencil.

Paula was anxious to get started so we hurried back down to our ponies. There was a practice area near the ring with an upright fence in the middle and we rode around it. 'I suppose we'd better take that fence. It'll soon be time for us to take part.' Her knees were trembling on the leather.

'Hi!' A girl on a grey Connemara reined in beside us.

'Oh, hi, Pam,' Paula introduced us. They had met at Pony Club rallies at the riding-school last year.

'Your pony's plaits are beautiful.' I must have sounded envious because she immediately said, 'Would you like me to do yours.' But I had no rubber bands.

Paula said, 'We'd better go,' moving off on Blackie.

Other riders were queueing with their ponies to take the practice jump and we joined them. First Pam's grey went, then Blackie. Bluebell cat-leaped it and I barely managed to stay in the saddle. The call came over the loudspeaker. 'Will those entered in the Clear Round Jumping competition, please go immediately to Pony Ring 2.'

'That's us!' Paula grabbed her reins. Her hands were shaking. We crowded the entrance to the ring waiting our turn. I waved to Mam and Dad who were standing by with Mrs Casey, Dan and Adrian.

It was Paula who got a fit of the giggles first. Soon neither of us could stop. I said, 'The jumps are small.'

'Yeah, but there are an awful lot of them,' and we burst into nervous giggles again.

'No 121, Woollongong Lad, owned and ridden by Paula Casey.'

Paula's knuckles were white on the reins as she rode Blackie into the arena. She set off at a good canter, facing him towards the brush fence. Here was a jump he was used to, having done it so often at home in our field. He thundered into it, and stopped. Paula hung over his head. Fixing herself in the saddle, she swung him about and headed him for it again. But again he refused. The steward shouted, 'Get him over it this time and you're in for a rosette.'

But Blackie had made up his mind. Suddenly, a figure out of the crowd came vaulting into the ring. It was Dad,

hurrying across to her, the steward following close behind. 'Hup!' They flapped their arms and ran behind Blackie who rolled the whites of his eyes at them and took off in a hurry. With some more encouragement, he cleared the next fence too. And the next. But at the last fence, the gate, before Dad could get there, he refused again, although Paula did finally get him over.

As she rode out of the arena, she looked over at the steward but his hand stayed firmly clamped on the lid of the rosette box.

There was no time to talk. It was my turn now. Bluebell set off at a slow trot and refused to break into a canter – I was just sitting there, listening to myself giggling. Going into the first jump, she slowed down even more. I faced her for the jump again. How could she act like this? There was the sound of running feet behind us. 'Hup!' With Dad at her heels, Bluebell jumped it from a standstill and to loud cheering Dad took the jump too.

I stopped feeling embarrassed. A strange feeling was growing inside me. I suddenly realised that she was depending on me to give her confidence, asking me what to do next and it was up to me, the rider, to give her the right signals. Armed with this new understanding I applied my legs and tightening my grip on the reins urged her on, eyes straight ahead on the next jump. Don't look down, look where you're going.

The single pole painted black and yellow with the sign 'Road Closed'. She came into it slowly, despite me pushing her, as if she were trying to read it. Then she lifted off and we were clear. She trotted into all the jumps, one, two, three jumps – a small spread, a line of hay bales, barrels. Last jump, the gate. She slowed, sensing my fear. The gate seemed narrow and I was afraid she would get stuck in it.

'Hup!' She poked her head over. 'Go on!' And she was over. A clear round!

Dad's long arm reached out and the steward handed over

a red rosette. Dad placed a handful of oats under Bluebell's muzzle and she blew away the chaff with her snorting.

'Can I go again?' Dad handed me the entry fee. Greatly encouraged by our first round, this time I was determined to have a clear round without Dad's help or anyone else's. While I was waiting, I looked around for Paula to show her my rosette but there was no sign of her. Then Bluebell whinnied happily. Blackie had moved up beside us, only this time was Adrian who was riding.

'Hold up, you brute.' Adrian jerked his head away from Bluebell and ground his teeth. 'He'll jump this time.'

My number was being called. This time, I forgot about all the people watching and thought only of one thing – guiding Bluebell over the jumps. I pushed her on with my legs and my seat. Up she trotted to the first jump, gathered herself, and we were over. On to the next one which was immediately facing us and again, pushing her on with my arms and legs and heels and seat, she cleared that too. Each jump she took in the same manner, approaching it slowly as if to check it out, then lifting up at the last minute. It was a jerky uncomfortable ride and it was very hard keeping her going, but at last we were over the gate and the steward was waving another rosette at us.

'Good girl. Good girl.' Patting her, shaking with pride. 'Dad, more oats.'

As he held the small sack for Bluebell, he kept an eye on Blackie in the ring, just in case help was needed. But a big change had come over that pony. He was flying over his jumps and in no time at all Adrian rode in for his rosette. I caught sight of Paula standing by the entrance and as Blackie came trotting through she turned away.

I forgot about her for a moment and looked for Dad. Where had he got to? I wanted to go around the jumps one more time for another rosette but needed the entry fee. Overhead the sky had grown dark, with heavy black clouds closing in around us. Big blobs fell on the saddle and soaked into it.

'Run! It's going to be a downpour!' The steward had called a halt to the competition and horses and riders were scattering in all directions for shelter. Spotting Paula riding Blackie to the far hedge I trotted in her direction.

'Not much shelter here!' I shouted to her. She looked over but didn't answer.

The raindrops were falling through the branches at our backs and Paula was getting full brunt of it, sitting on Blackie where there was no shelter at all. She just sat there, eyes fixed on the pummel of the saddle as it came lashing down. Licking the drips coming off the peak of my cap I said, 'Hard luck you didn't win a rosette.' I tried to sound sad as I patted Bluebell's steaming streaming neck.

A chill wind whipped through the hedge. Paula pointed to the open field in front of us and her voice sounded cold. 'I'm going over there on my own to exercise. Blackie will be on his own in the next competition and he will need to get used to it. He's too dependant on Bluebell's company.'

'I don't think so,' I was thinking how nice it was that Blackie and Bluebell were such good friends. But then, anyone would have to like Bluebell. 'Wasn't she great?' I rubbed the rain off her flanks and it dropped in sheets. 'I never thought she'd jump the gate.'

'Blackie should have done better. He never goes well in the first round.'

'She did it first time out.' I patted her again.

'It wasn't his first time out.' Paula's voice was small and icy. 'You know he's jumped loads of times before.'

'Sorry, I was talking about Bluebell.'

'There's no need to go on about her.' Paula was looking straight ahead, lips tight.

I stopped patting Bluebell and suddenly realised how wet we were. The rain was trickling down my neck and back and had soaked through our jackets and jodhpurs, even into our boots. For a while neither of us spoke, then

Bluebell's head went up. Dad was approaching.

'There's a change of clothes for you in the car and something to eat. Paula, you coming with us?' He kept the umbrella out of the way of the ponies.

'No, thanks.' Paula muttered something about having a change in her own car and rode off.

Bluebell was still shivering, and on Dad's advice I trotted her about and hopped over a few bales to warm her. Paula was galloping away in the distance.

Later, when it had cleared and I got to the caravan to enter in the local class competition, we met up again. She was entering too and she frowned when she saw me.

She was still speaking in a peculiar voice. 'There's no point in the two of us entering in the same class,' she said. 'You can go in the one for ponies under 128cms and I'll go in the under 138cms.'

'But Paula, I'd prefer to go in the one you're going in. It would be better fun.' What was wrong with her all of a sudden?

'We'd better not,' she said. 'We're rivals in the ring. We'd be competing against each other.' Her face was tight, as if she were going to explode.

In this competition, Bluebell was supposed to go through the different paces of walking, trotting and cantering. She was too tired so I didn't ask her. But she executed the figure eight really well. We were placed ninth, really second last. But I was well pleased to be getting another rosette to hang on my bedroom wall, a white 'Special' this time.

Paula's competition was next and she was placed eighth out of nine. Looking more cheerful, she rode over to show me her 'Special' before securing it on Blackie's bridle, beside the red rosette already put there by Adrian.

The judges' umbrellas were going up once more so we headed our ponies towards the loading area.

Mrs Casey was already there with Adrian and Dan. 'Cheer up, darling,' she said to Paula. 'Better luck next

time. We all have our little disappointments but we just
have to learn to live with them.

Adrian was leading Blackie up the ramp and he turned
around. 'You know, Paula, you're not going to get anywhere
with that pony unless you toughen up, be more like me.
You're too soft. What he needs is plenty of the stick!'

Dan blurted out, 'If you had ridden Blackie in the first
round, you wouldn't have done any better.'

'Aw, shut up. What would you know?' swinging around
threateningly. And then something funny happened. He
stumbled on the ramp and fell. There was silence.
Redfaced, he scrambled up out of the fresh dung and
glared at Blackie before taking a swipe at him with the lead
rope.

In the back seat on the way home, we held our noses,
glancing sideways at each other behind Adrian's back.

From Paula's house, I set off for home at a trot, in a
hurry to 'phone Grandad and tell him how Bluebell had
won three rosettes and would possibly have won a fourth,
another red one, but for that thunder shower.

Dad was waiting at the gate, As we came in, he said, 'You
know, Sarah, your pony looked so much thinner than the
other ponies at the Show today. You'd think she had been
starved. She has put on very little condition since we got
her. I think we'll change her into the big field tonight. The
grass is much better there.'

Just what Bluebell needs, I thought, as I led her into the
field. 'Easy, Bluebell!' She started as a single magpie flut-
tered out of the bushes and disappeared into the oak tree.

'That you, Dad?' Lying in bed, one eye open, not able to
sleep because of this fluttery feeling. 'Dad, could you get a
worm dose for Bluebell tomorrow?'

He sat on the side of the bed. 'Won't you be going to The
Square on Saturday. You'll be able to pick it up then, yourself. I've enough to do.'

'But, Dad, I was wondering if you could get it tomorrow. Grandad did say that it should be done immediately. And he mentioned it again this evening. He said she was probably infested with the worms.'

Dad got off the bed. 'I'll call to Barry's tomorrow and get the dose. You know, Sarah, that pony is in your care and I hope you realise that you've been rather careless. That is a matter you should have dealt with months ago.'

That night I had a bad dream. It was about Paula's Blackie. He was buried to his neck in quicksand and when I came again to look, the flesh was eaten away and all that remained was a skull.

8 TROUBLE

Next morning I ran out before breakfast, to the big field. The air was warm and yellow-bright and the birds were singing in the soft green hedges and trees. Bluebell was so perfect yesterday that I wanted to thank her and tell her how lucky I was to have her as my own pony. The four rosettes were already packed in my schoolbag to show off to my friends.

But as soon as I turned into the big field, I knew something was wrong. There was no whinny of greeting. She was pacing about sadly, pawing the ground. I walked towards her and then began to run, my heart thumping loudly. Within seconds of reaching her I heard myself cry out in terror as she suddenly collapsed in front of me and began to thresh about. As well as paddling with her front legs she was now banging her head off the ground.

'Stop it. Get up, Bluebell!' My voice was high and rising. I slapped her on the rump and she got up. Just in time I jumped out of her way as she lay down again, this time on her other side, still throwing her head about.

I screamed at her to get up and she did.

Running for the house, my stomach gave a heave.

Mam quickly dried her hands. 'We'd better get the vet.' After looking up the Golden Pages she telephoned a number in Rathcoole. 'He's coming right away,' she put down the receiver. 'He says it might be colic. We've got to get her up and keep her moving until he gets here.'

Bluebell was lying on her side but we managed to get her to her feet again and walk her around on the headcollar.

'The pain must be going,' Mam said brightly. 'She's not

as agitated. Maybe there was no need to call the vet at all. She must have eaten too much.'

Looking at Bluebell's bloodshot eyes, I wondered. Somehow I felt she was even sicker than before.

'How long has she been like this?' The vet was examining her, listening to her heart with his stethoscope. I threw some oats on the grass but she made no effort to pick at them, just stood there with her head down.

When I told him, he folded away his stethoscope slowly, hands shaking slightly.

'Watch out!' Suddenly Bluebell swayed and almost fell on top of him as she threw herself to the gound again in agony. Recovering his balance he went to his medicine case and drew out two syringefuls of brown liquid. After swabbing Bluebell's neck he injected her slowly into the vein. I knew by the look on his face that my pony must be very sick.

He turned to Mam, hands deep in the pockets of of his old tweed jacket. 'I'm afraid, Mrs Quinn, your pony has a very bad case of colic. I've given her the strongest painkiller and if it is a simple colic pain she should improve within two hours. Ring me at eleven o'clock if she's not better.'

On the way back to the house he was talking earnestly with Mam. I didn't listen. I tried to think only of yesterday and the four beautiful rosettes in the bottom of my bag.

When he had left, Mam returned with my schoolbag. 'If there is any development I'll ring you.'

Paula wasn't in: Dan said she had a bad headache. Sitting on the bench I remembered the paragraph in the pony manual that said colic was an abdominal pain, similar to human stomach-ache. Could be very serious. This last line kept churning about in my stomach.

Babs came over. 'Babs, I think my pony is dying.'

Her eyes widened, then narrowed to pinholes of light. 'Well, she had a disease, hadn't she?'

'Please come down to see her after school.'

'I'll try.' She sauntered off with Katie again. Then she shouted back, 'Don't worry, the knackers will give you something for her.'

Niall and Trevor overheard and gathered round. Niall assured me, 'She'll get better. Lots of horses get colic and survive.'

Trevor said, 'It's probably a twisted gut. My father had a horse once that died of it.'

'The vet was back.' In the kitchen, Dad's voice was grim. Mam was biting her lip and twisting the ring on her finger. 'We've bad news for you, Sarah. Bluebell has a twisted gut. She could have an operation but it would be very expensive, with no guarantee of success.'

I watched his fingers make furrows in his hair. 'I'm sorry but we just couldn't afford it. She may have to be put down. I'm sorry.' His voice was hard and his fingers kept raking.

Mam's voice sounded far-away. 'Dad and I were just saying that we would go to Connemara Pony Show next

August and buy you a new filly. A registered Connemara this time, that you could school and break yourself, get ready for the shows and for your school team.'

'I want Bluebell.' I heard my voice, quietly determined, and the floor lurched again.

There was the sound of barking outside. A white car pulled up in front of the house and two people got out. Dad and Mam took a step towards me but I was out before them. My arms were tight about Bluebell as they approached.

'Sarah,' the old vet said softly, 'I brought this young man along to give a second opinion. He's a horse specialist, just returned from Kentucky, and on his way back to the veterinary hospital. I persuaded him to come here. Seeing as I'm his old father, he couldn't refuse, could he? He's going to have a look at Bluebell. I'd like to know what he thinks.'

My arms relaxed a little.

'Steady there,' the young vet spoke to Bluebell in a soothing voice. 'Let's have a look at you, pet.'

Bluebell turned, as if she knew what he was saying, her eyes pleading for relief.

His beard danced in the breeze as he examined her, looking at her eyes, talking and humming a tune. He turned to me. His face was grave and his eyes grew wider.

'Dinny Quinn . . . you're his granddaughter aren't you?' How is he keeping? And this must be the little pony he mentioned to me that night. See, I haven't forgotten!'

He beckoned me away from the others. 'Sarah, I'm afraid your pony has a very bad case of gut entrapment. I'll have to get her to the horse hospital right away.'

'We can't,' I said. 'Dad hasn't got the money.'

'Listen,' Chris Beresford looked at me solemnly. 'I owe your grandfather for something. This is on me. But I must operate before it's too late. Have you got a horse-box? No? Not to worry!'

On the small mobile telephone I heard his request for the

horse ambulance and the precise instructions. When I mentioned the worm dose, he said, 'That might have done it all right.' He explained how the pony could have been undernourished because of the worm infestation and this had prevented her from digesting the rich grass, causing her gut to become trapped, only he had some other name for it. 'It needs to be freed immediately or it will kill her.'

'Look here,' Dad went over to Chris, 'I know you mean well, but we've already decided. We can't pay for this operation.'

'Don't worry,' said Chris airily. 'It's is already paid for.'

He gave Bluebell a sedative and some pain-killers.

The horse ambulance arrived and a girl in overalls jumped out. Chris introduced her as Tess, his head nurse, then said, 'I'll go on ahead and prepare for the operation.'

I went with Bluebell in the ambulance, Mam and Dad were to follow on.

Bluebell was quiet on the journey but it was a relief to see the hospital at last, a long low building set in the fields. Chris was outside waiting. 'I'll give her a full clinical examination, just to confirm my earlier diagnosis.'

Bluebell was led into the building and put into a stall. When he was finished his examination, Chris gave the nurses instructions and they hurried off. 'It's as I thought,' he told me. 'Your pony has an entrapment of the large gut that must be untangled and put right by rotation. This procedure is non-surgical. There will be no wounds or stitches but she must have a general anaesthetic and due to her weak condition there is no certainty that it will save her, but at least she will have a chance.'

'She's not in any pain,' I said. 'Can't you just leave her?'

'The fact that she has no pain means the condition is critical.'

Numbly I followed Bluebell into the Knockdown Box, a padded green room, and waited while the nurse fitted her with rubber boots. 'Just so she won't injure herself when she's going down with the anaesthetic.'

She directed me to where I could watch the operation through a glass porthole in the door of the operating theatre. Through it I saw the huge syringe moving in Bluebell's direction. She started to sway and moments later her knees buckled and she fell heavily to the padded floor.

My stomach lurched. I couldn't watch any more. I ran to the cloakroom where I wiped my face with a tissue. At Reception, a little dog was wandering about, wanting someone to play with him. His golf ball had rolled under the couch and I poked it clear. He ran off.

I sat there for a while, utterly alone. Where *was* everyone when I needed them – Paula and Niall and Babs? Now I had no friend. I knew Bluebell was dead.

I looked up. Tess was standing there. 'Your pony is now in the recovery box. Would you like to go down and see her? Your friends are there.' And she led the way. 'We kept her in the operating theatre for fifteen minutes or so until she recovered from the anaesthetic and was able to walk.'

I couldn't believe it! She was alive!

Slowly my leg started to hop. 'Is she okay?' was all I could say.

She smiled. 'Everything is fine. The operation has been a success.'

'Has she many stitches?'

Her eyebrows went up. 'Didn't Chris explain it was non-surgical?'

'I don't remember . . . how did they do it? No, I don't want to know.'

Paula and Niall were with her. Niall was patting her nose. She gave a small whinny when she saw me.

'You had just gone when we arrived,' said Paula.

Niall said, 'She's fine. Not a bother on her. We were beginning to wonder where you were.'

Tess seemed very pleased when Paula pointed to the

small hard droppings that Bluebell had passed. 'Good.' She entered this in on her chart and explained that the droppings meant that the gut was now open again and working. 'I'll prepare her a mash.'

'Where are Mam and Dad?'

'They're looking for Chris. Here they come.'

Chris came striding in. His sleeves were rolled up and he smelled of horse dung. I wanted to pump his hand and tell him what a great day this was, the greatest day of my life because of the wonderful miracle he worked – resurrecting Bluebell from the dead. Instead I just stood there grinning. He examined the chart intently, then nodded. 'We'll keep her here for a few days' observations although I don't think there will be any complications. She's a hardy little pony. Tomorrow you can lead her out on the lawn here to graze.'

For a second, the thought that she might be lonely crossed my mind. But she looked quite comfortable in the deep bed of shavings.

Dad was at the door. He stepped inside. 'Look, Chris,' he began, 'what you did was marvellous. We don't know how to thank you.' Mam was grinning like mad behind him, dabbing at eyes that were red-rimmed.

As if Bluebell knew what was going on, she shuffled up and stuck her head out over Chris' left shoulder, letting it rest there with a big snort of contentment. Everyone laughed only Chris who said, 'There's my reward. See, I've made a new friend,' and he rubbed the pony's muzzle.

Tess came to the door. 'Chris, that mare and foal are on the way.'

'Be right there.' He gave Bluebell a last pat and went out humming.

Niall was rubbing his stomach. 'What's the matter, Niall?' Mam was at his side, her voice full of concern, looking at him as though he too had a colic.

'I'm hungry,' he mumbled.

'So am I,' Paula added.

As we drove off for a take-away, Niall said enthusiastically. 'I saw it all. Bluebell was hitched on to a big block and tackle, then they bowled her right over. Of course, if I'd been in there I'd have rolled her over myself. You need to be strong for a job like that. Still, it was a very neat job. I hate blood. He stuck his hand right in under the tail into the ...'

'The back passage,' Paula grinned.

'Yeah, the back passage,' Niall went on. 'And he unravelled the gut by twisting her one way and his hand the other way.'

'Oh, come on, mate!' Paula poked him in the ribs. 'Give over. Sarah doesn't want to hear any more about Bluebell's operation. We're going to eat, remember.'

We all laughed.

Mate, she called him. I thought, maybe that's what we were, Paula, Niall and I. Good mates.

This was a great day for Bluebell and me, and I was not going to forget it. And I would never be sad again because I would always remember this day.

And Babs? Well, she and Paula were still my best friends. She was just in very bad humour for the last while, that's all. Now that Bluebell was well, I'd forgiven her. She couldn't have meant what she said, about the knackers and all.

Over the next two days, Mam drove me to the hospital after school and I stayed until teatime, helping Tess to look after the mare and foals and popping in and out to Bluebell. To tell the truth, I don't think she missed me. She had taken a fancy to the gelding next door and they spent most of the day nickering softly to one another.

The day she went home, Mam left an envelope for Chris at reception. It was a donation towards his expenses, she said, but would not tell me what was in it.

9 GRANDAD

In the warm sunshine, pear and apple trees hung green over walls, bending low with heavy crops, Grass ripened early in rainless fields. And in the garden, blackcurrants and gooseberry fruits clustered on the bushes.

Every day Bluebell grew bigger and stronger, feasting on the rich grass. Her once muddy coat had quickly turned a glossy dark grey, with silver feather showing through it here and there. With her strong neck and body she was no longer the skinny, miserable pony Grandad had bought, but a sturdy mare.

The summer holidays are coming nearer and but for Mam I could be having a brilliant time. She gets very fussy about my school examinations, revision and stuff like that. It's not fair.

Bluebell is basking outside in the warm breeze, sometimes grazing, sometimes rolling lazily, and here am I bent over my copybook with a crippling pain in my back.

And while I'm here slaving at unimportant things, my pony grows fat and bored in the field for want of attention. Paula has just called for me to go riding with her, but Mam would not give in. Paula is lucky. Her mother actually says, 'You're studying too hard, Paula. Saddle up and get out into the fresh air.' Such a difference in mothers!

'Sarah, are you nearly finished?' Mam put her head around the door, voice impatient. 'Grandad is on his way. We're to meet him off the bus in Maynooth at six-thirty.'

The bus was there before us, and Grandad was sitting on the window-sill of Spicer's Bakery, big black hat shading him from the sun, hands folded over the crook of his cane stick, brown boots firmly planted on the tarmacadam, brown zipper bag resting between them.

'Grandad!' the force of my mighty hug almost pulled him off his seat. 'The car is in the square. I'll carry your bag.'

'Sure there's nothing in it. Only me shoes and a pair of clean socks. And me oul pyjamas.' He looked at me suddenly. 'You're growing like a rush!'

Trouble is, I can't help thinking that Grandad has shrunk.

'That oul bus had me crippled.' He dropped his bag to tell us. 'The driver stopped at Harry's in Kinnegad but I didn't get out. You know those fellows? They're always in a hurry. I'd be afraid he'd take off without me.'

As we whizzed along the by-road, he chortled, 'You know what I'm going to tell you? This is great country around here. The west of Ireland isn't a patch on it! Not a patch! Look at those fine fields.' His voice changed in disgust. 'Cabbage gardens. That's all we have in the west. Cabbage gardens!'

Mam slowed so that he could get a good look at the trees and hedges, the wide rolling fields. 'And no houses. No people!' he exclaimed. 'And no stock! The west of Ireland must be producing for the whole country.'

At our gate, Mam passed him his walking-stick and we got out. 'Did you notice I got a bit bad in the walk?' Without waiting an answer he strode on ahead, eager, one thing on his mind. Bluebell, I thought.

He stopped at the sight of our new jumping arena, his mouth in a wide 'O' of amazement. 'It's like a Ballsbridge course! Or Millstreet.'

'We'll be jumping them later on,' I promised, one eye on Mam behind us. He especially admired our latest additions, a new fence of hay bales and a small timber gate which Dad had made, also an old mattress and a table-top.

Bluebell was at the lower end of the field and raised her

head when she heard the voices. As Grandad approched, she stood with ears pricked in curiosity. Then giving a soft whinny of welcome, she took a step in our direction. This made him a very happy man.

'She knew me. Imagine that.' His voice was full of gratitude as she came trotting up to us. 'Get me a pick of grass, Sarah.' With a quick daintiness, she nuzzled it off his hand.

'Grandad!' Dad was coming towards us, in his crumpled suit. 'You're looking well!'

Grandad was getting livelier by the minute. 'You didn't cut the bit of hay yet, Shane? Cut it right away. The weather is up. First-crop hay is great for a pony.' An energetic wave of his stick sent Bluebell obediently trotting off, moving smartly. 'Was it a twisted gut she had? The very same as Desert Orchid. That Chris Beresford is a great man. Any other vet would have her put down . . . You know what I'm going to do for that man. I'm going to call a reel after him. The Chris Beresford reel. How does that sound? Pity he's away, but you tell him, Sarah, sometime that he has a reel called after him and a damn fine wan too.'

Bluebell came trotting down towards us again. 'Will you be saddling her up soon? although I suppose we'll have the tea first. There should be a great lep in her.'

I rubbed my sweaty palms on my jeans. What if she can't jump. We hadn't jumped her since her operation.

'We'll have the tea first.' Dad steered us inside.

Through the open door, down into the paddock to nest in the cool fresh grass and I lay there until my heart stopped thumping. I was nervous.

Bluebell's high whinny caused me to scramble to my feet. Hoofbeats could be heard on the road outside. I waved to Grandad who was making his way into the paddock.

He spotted Paula at the gate.

'Who's this coming? It must be your friend. Babs, isn't it?'

'No, Grandad, Babs is my other best friend, this is Paula. Do you remember I told you she was coming down for a riding-lesson?'

'She's the girl you go riding with. I'd prefer her to the other one.'

'I'd better go and get the tack.'

'Right. I'll be catching the pony.'

When I came back out, he was clutching Bluebell by the bob and he and Paula were chatting away.

'We think he's pretty old but we don't know for certain,' Paula was saying.

He let go of Bluebell and opened Blackie's mouth.

'Hmmmm'. There was the sound of a loud snap. 'There should be a good lep in him . . . have you no saddle?' I noticed then that Paula was riding bareback.

'It's gone in for repairs. It's falling apart. The saddler gave it to me when the owner didn't collect it.' I'm hoping they've forgotten about it by now.'

We started to giggle but Grandad waved his stick, all ready for action. 'Go on there now, till I see ye!'

With a twirl of his walking-stick, he walked smartly into the centre of the field and stood there watching us as we rode around him. Then he nodded his head and beckoned with his finger. This was only the warm-up. Soon he was waving his arms about and the instructions came rapidly. 'Shoulders back! Don't slouch! Are you going to take off or what? Walk! Trrrrot! Canter on!'

His methods were very different from Mrs M at the riding-school, but his results were even better. Whatever about Bluebell, I'd never had to work so hard in my life.

Grandad's arm churned one way to show us the direction to go, then as we took off, he pivoted, shouted, and pointed in the opposite direction. Blackie crashed past Bluebell with a nose to spare.

After that he cautioned us, head shaking, finger wagging at us. 'Stop there now. Let me see you take a few hops.'

Paula was panting. 'You go first,' she breathed. I managed to swerve clear of Blackie's hind quarters and went in front. But Blackie was not pleased with that arrangement. He tried to catch up. The ponies collided but recovered balance and staggered over the jump.

Grandad yelled, 'Don't do that. It's dangerous! The other way, Paula, the other way,' using his elbows as if he were driving the jeep. Then he shouted, 'Stop!' calling us over to him. He pulled and offered grass to our astonished ponies. 'They needed that bit of limbering up. Well, okay, just give them one more hop.'

Walking briskly to the pole and barrel fence, he dropped his walking-stick and caught one of the barrels, then the other, setting them upright and resting the pole on top. Then he picked up his stick again and waved it, breathing hard. 'Now, hop that. From this side.' In slow motion, his free hand circled to show us from which side we were to take it.

Paula looked at me, face tense with fear under the brim. 'The last time I attempted at that height, Blackie crashed into the jump and I went flying. And I haven't even got a saddle today!'

'I'm nervous,' I said.

'Come on now! Don't let the ponies get cold. Take it this way.' Grandad's arm was circling again.

'Which way does he mean?' hissed Paula.

'Okay, Sarah first,' shouted Grandad. 'Check her now, and then on the last three strides let her go and pop over!'

Bluebell cleared it easily.

'Now, Paula,' Grandad shouted again. 'Hold him in, keep your legs on him. Then go with him!'

Blackie swept over the pole.

'That will do. That will do. Give them a bit of a rest now.'

He stood to attention between the two ponies, offering wisps of grass to their hanging heads. 'Bluebell has the

makings of a good jumper,' he said. 'Blackie, too. And ye're topping little riders.'

One glance at Paula told that she felt as I did, a mixture of pride and hope and delight in her face. Just as if he had awarded us joint first prize.

But Grandad was peering closely at Blackie. 'He's a fine lepper, only . . . ' The sun glinted on his glasses. 'Did I see him trying to veer away from the fence as he came in? Aha!' He thumped his stick on the ground. 'I thought so! You'll have to get him out of that bad habit.'

'Yeah, well,' Paula's voice had gone a little flat, 'He's inclined to run out when he puts down his head. We have to get a tougher bit for him. I'm just using a snaffle at the moment.'

Grandad, saying nothing, began to rummage in his pocket. He held up two pieces of baler twine and set to work, tying them to both rings of Blackie's bit and securing them loosely to the little rings above each stirrup leather. 'There, that'll give you more control.' The stick waved again. 'Off ye go again!'

This time, Paula led the way and we cleared it once more.

'That'll do now.' His voice carried across to us. 'Your ponies have enough.' They were sweating under us, so we got off to give them a rest.

'Blackie has the power in his front legs whereas Bluebell has it in the back ones,' He looked approvingly at them.

Puffing a little, Paula patted Blackie. Her pony gave Grandad a sidelong glance while Bluebell let out a huge sigh.

'We'll do it again tomorrow.' he promised. But that evening he was examining the sky. 'We're in for fine weather. That's a great sky. Not a sign of rain on it.' He tested the wind with his finger. 'And the wind is from the right point. I'd better go home early tomorrow and get the hay cut.'

When Paula came over the next day. I told her he had gone.

'He always says, *Níl aon tinteán mar do thínteán féin*, He never stays longer than a day. Next time he says he'll bring up a few rosettes in his pocket and he'll have a fiver for the winner.'

Paula was disappointed. 'Just think,' her voice was sad. 'He gives us the riding-lesson, then pays us for entertaining him.'

10 SUMMER HOLIDAYS

Sweet smells of new cut hay drifted in through the open window as the warm breeze rustled through the elderberry and honeysuckle and delicate wild roses in the hedges. In full flood of bright sunshine, Bluebell rhythmically unfolded her silver tail at the light wash of sound from the dual carriageway which wafted up the hill and hovered over the music of her peaceful unhurried munching.

The first day of the school holidays and the whole summer stretched out before us. Freedom! I hopped up on Bluebell's bare back and rode her down into the hayfield at a fast canter, taking her over the stubble, along by the elderberry hedges, under the oak-tree, lifting her over the swards in our path. The evening scent of hawthorn and woodbine in the ditches blended with the sweet smell of hay and horse dung as my pony carried me away under the red evening sun.

'Go, Bluebell!' In response, she burst into a gallop, sharing my sense of carefree delight. We were no longer held by the boundaries of the field. We were pacing across the golden sands of the Arabian desert, well ahead of the pursuing palace guards, stolen gold and silver in our saddlebags, Bluebell fully aware of the need to outrun our captors. Pressed low in the saddle to avoid the constant shower of poisoned arrows, I left all choice of speed and direction to my trusty steed.

We had reached our oasis, the oak-tree and the ropes of the swing coming back into focus. The big sun rested on the side of the hill as we floated from the golden light of the field into the shadow of the hedge and out again, rays gleaming through Bluebell's silver mane and her tail spread behind her as we rose and sank in glimmerings of light above the shiny strands of woven hay.

'Let's take a jump, Bluebell.'

The stacked bales made a natural jump and I gave her her head, letting her canter into them. Suddenly cold with horror I saw the tractor mower on the other side. There was nothing I could do. We were airborne – that's far too wide – she'd never make that stretch – I gave that extra squeeze, felt the surge of strength beneath me and the stretch of her legs.

We had cleared the bales, blade and all. I got down. 'Good girl!' hugging her fiercely, only now realising what Grandad meant when he said that once I had earned her friendship, she would not let me down. I hoped I would never lose that friendship.

As soon as my legs were ready to obey me again, I hurried inside.

That night, wearing just a T-shirt, I stood at my bedroom window in the darkness. It was too hot for sleep. Along the floor of the valley, a web of yellow lights winked their way under the curtain of city haze. All was quiet and peaceful, except for the faint clink of a horse's shoe. Automatically I turned my head to look over by the wall of the house where she often stood at night for company and I saw her dark outline in the moonlight, the shape of her head.

I yawned, and was about to make my way back to bed when some other movement caught my eye. Only briefly did she appear distinct from the other larger shadow by her side. I waited, and just as I was sure that this second figure was a reflection of light on the glass, the two shadows separated again. This time, their two heads crossed and they began to lick one another, massaging each other on the neck with long sweeping strokes and this continued in silent rhythm until the moon quenched and it was too dark to see any more. I got back into the bed. What had happened was as soft and silent as a dream and I fell into a restful sleep.

'I'm glad we're going to Pony Camp,' Paula lay on her tummy on the studio couch, forms spread out in front of her, long brown legs waving in the air. 'We need that experience if we're to qualify for the School Cross-Country Team.'

'What is a cross-country anyway?' I asked. A slight tremble had developed in one leg and my foot drummed lightly on the oak chest where I was sitting. 'I don't know if Bluebell would really be into that.'

'It's a trail of various fences over a long distance. The object is to complete the course in a certain time. It's very unusual for it to be based on the fastest speed, because that would be dangerous. Usually you are given a set time and you have to do your round as close to that as possible. A refusal means ten penalties. It's all done on penalties. Let's say if you have a refusal and come in ten seconds too fast, well then, you have earned a penalty of twenty seconds, which means you wouldn't stand a chance of winning.'

It sounded very complicated. I said, 'I doubt if Bluebell would be very good at it.'

'On the contrary, it would suit Bluebell and Blackie very well. You get a lot of crazy ponies racing around with their riders clinging on and they come in maybe two minutes too fast. Their ponies are too good. Now, let's just concentrate on Pony Camp for the moment, shall we?'

'Sure.' I felt so grown up when Paula was around. I peered over her shoulder as she read the forms.

'Hey!' Paula's forehead had divided in two with a frown. 'Wait a minute, you can't enter your pony if he's very old.'

'Anything in the conditions that says you can't join if your pony is too young?' flopping down beside her. Paula was stabbing the form with her index finger. 'And it says here too that you have to send on the money for Pony Club and Pony Camp with the entry for Pony Camp. I won't have enough. My pocket-money goes on straw and nuts for Blackie at the moment.'

'Can't your mam pay for you?'

Paula shook her head. 'Mum says the building industry is in a bad patch just now. Irish people won't pay architects.'

'Couldn't you get a loan or something?' My money was coming from a loan got from Dad, repayable at Christmas.

Paula shook her head. 'It would be ages before I could pay her back and I still owe her for my new jodhpurs.'

'You'd probably have preferred if you had stayed on in Australia where you'd have more money.' More money, I thought, and more friends. Not just me. But I didn't say it, trying not to feel let down.

Her light blue eyes had dark veins, like spiders' webs. But when she laughed they disappeared into bright crinkles. 'Fair dinkum! Give us a go!'

'Hey! That accent is brill.' I was glad my voice sounded cheerful. I wished she preferred living in Ireland where she had me as a friend, even if the money was difficult.

Her forehead creased again. 'Well, I did like it there, until my dad got killed.'

'What happened to him?'

'A premature explosives blast at work. It happened about two years ago.'

'Do you miss him?'

'Dunno. Didn't know him very well. He was away a lot. I guess. Mum does, though. It's not easy rearing three children on her pay.'

There was a short silence while I watched the light shine through the sunflowers on the red curtains. I said, 'Hey, my teacher was doing a song about a man at a mine who was blasted into the sky so far that the time was "docked" from his pay.' Noisily clearing my throat, curling of the lip upwards:

Every morning at seven o'clock
There's twenty tarriers aworking at the rock,
And the boss comes along and he says 'Keep still
And come down heavy with the cast-iron drill.'
Drill, ye tarriers, drill,
Drill, ye tarriers, drill.

'Well,' Paula was fidgeting with the forms, 'we didn't get proper compensation because he hadn't followed the regulations or something. Then Mum was depressed and the doctor advised her to go back to Ireland. Anyway I prefer it here. I hate the beach and swimming.' Clatter of a bucket outside. I lay back in relief, a comfortable knob of warmth melting and spreading about my insides. So she preferred living here, after all. I was her friend.

I sprang up. Paula *had* to come to Pony Camp with me. Already I was reaching for my runners. 'We'll get the money. No problem. I've a great idea. C'mon.'

'Hey, where are you going?'

'Over to Babs'.'

A figure in red was bobbing about the back garden. She seemed to be on her own. When she saw us she abandoned the builder's cement-mixer she was playing with and came racing towards us. A muffed scream came from somewhere behind her but Babs kept going.

'We're starting a new club. You and Katie can be in it.'

Katie! Her eyes travelled to the cement-mixer and she grinned at us. 'I'll be back in a minute,' and ran off.

The engine noise stopped and Katie's head popped out of the mixer drum.

'What kind of a club?' Babs was back.

'It'll be like a club for sending someone for a big operation. Or going to the moon even,' I explained. 'We all pay in our money. Paula goes to Pony Camp and we go places with whatever money is left.'

Babs' face was beaming like a full moon. It always does

that when there is a brilliant idea floating around.

'Where will we have our meetings?' Paula asked.

'What about the . . .' A quick look from Babs and I remembered in time that the ranch house was a secret between the two of us.

When we had dusted Katie down, the four of us walked

back through the fields. In the hot sunshine we kept to the shade of the leafy hedges, the long grass tickling our bare legs.

'We'll put all our pocket-money into the club every week,' I told them. 'Then, before the end of the holidays, we'll all go on a picnic and a swim to the canal – after we've paid for Paula to join the Pony Club,' I added.

Babs picked a dandelion in the grass and swished it through the air, eyes big and black with excitement. Katie, still feeling wonky after her churning in the mixer, looked grumpy and complained at every step. Now she said, 'If we go on the picnic, Babs and me will have to cycle.'

How did Babs stick her!

And when Paula said she couldn't pay any money into the club, Katie had to object, 'And why shouldn't Paula have to pay?'

'Because,' I was trying not to yell, even though it was not easy to have patience with such a dumb-dumb, 'the money is for her, isn't it?'

We climbed through the brambles and mounted the ditch. The sun shone warmly down on the bank and the grass was silky under our hands and knees. Paula went first, carefully removing a briar from her shorts and holding it clear for Katie. They went on over the ridge. Babs, directly in front of me, was slowing up, taking her time. I went to pass her.

'Wait.' Head low she plucked a daisy, twiddling it between her thumb and forefinger.

We rested on the grassy slope enjoying a cool breeze and pulling the daisies, sprinkling the petals around.

'Sarah,' when Babs spoke, her voice was low and dreamy. 'Do you remember the time me and you were best friends?'

'Yeah,' I pulled another petal. Love, like, hate, adore, friendship. 'When we used to be building our club-houses and ranch houses.' It seemed a long time ago.

The daisy petals drifted lazily down. Not looking at me, Babs said again, 'Do you remember the time Joe and Edel tried to bury us alive in the tunnel we made in Clinton's? When they blocked up the entrance and we had to dig ourselves out, with big rocks collapsing down on us even though it was dark an' all?'

'Yeah. And I remember the first time you came to my house, you were only three. Do you remember? I came out and found you crying in the grass.'

'Yeah,' she answered.

We said nothing more, only looking down on to the path we had travelled through the fields from Babs' house, a path made by us long years ago, ever since we were only three. Now, the growth of briars and brambles and ferns

had almost closed it off. Butterflies and grasshoppers roared
past. A small wind caused the grass blades to bend and our
ditch fell into a shadow.

'Sarah. We were waiting for you!' Paula's figure stood on
the top of the ditch, hands on hips, Katie beside her.

I got to my feet. 'C'mon, Babs, we'd better go on.'

Babs got up, giving Paula a very unfriendly eye.

The inside of the tool-shed was dark and musty. We all sat
on an old wooden box, apart from Katie who stood at the
big door, keeping it open.

'We'd better start.' Paula lightly tapped her pencil on a
piece of paper. 'Who is going to be leader?'

This was going to be the hardest thing to agree on.

Katie got in quickly. 'I vote for Babs,' she said. But Paula
was busily tearing up paper. 'We'd better have a proper vote
on it, by secret ballot.' She passed around the paper and we
took the pencil in turn.

She counted the votes. Babs and I had got two votes
each. Katie and I had voted for Babs. My votes had come
from Paula and Babs. Babs was looking across at me, eyes
narrowed, and I knew there was no way she would ever
allow me be the leader. That I was sure of. And there was
no way I was going to let her, either. I said, 'I propose Paula
as leader. After all, the money is for her.'

'I second that.' Paula briskly tapped the pencil off her
teeth. 'When do we start collecting the money?'

A whine came from the door. 'When are we going to have
our picnic?'

'Yeah.' Babs was jumping up and down off her seat. 'Our
picnic. Where will we go?' Her black pupils were enormous
and I could feel the excitement rising, rising like the dust
under my drumming foot. 'Maybe we'll go some place really far away.'

There was a hush. Then Paula got up suddenly. 'What
about the bottom of the hill,' voice dry, the sound of her

pencil vibrating among the timbers as she strolled to the far corner of the shed.

Babs shuffled her feet. Ignoring her, she said to me, 'Do you remember the time me and you cycled on the Girl Guides outing?'

'Yeah, and you fell off at the bridge and you were calling, "Sarah, help me!" ' Our giggles filled the half darkness.

'Watch the door!' Babs yelled.

'We'll go further,' I promised. 'We'll go sixteen miles. We might even go to the sea!'

Katie suddenly let go of the door. In the darkness, Babs was the first to speak. 'I'd need to bring my swimsuit.'

'I'm not allowed go in deep water.' Katie was tugging at the door, stumbling over shovels and spades.

'Yippee!' The yell from Babs suddenly filled the darkness of the shed and I couldn't sit still any longer either. All at once we were jumping about and falling over timbers and shouting and yelling and clutching at each other and rolling on the floor.

'Stop it! You're raising dust.' Paula was standing in the lighted doorway looking crossly at us. Katie, at her side, suddenly gave a great big sneeze and that set us off laughing again. Seeing the look on Paula's face I tried to pull Babs on to the seat, wiping my eyes at the same time.

Paula kept tapping her pencil. 'Let's continue the meeting.' But Babs wouldn't sit down. 'When are we going on the picnic?' throwing an angry eye at Paula.

'In a few weeks.' I looked at Paula, hoping she'd agree.

But she was checking the date on her watch. 'We won't have the money by then.'

Babs was still for a moment, 'I might be able to get some more.'

'Where?' Katie's nose was twitching.

Babs didn't answer. But she and I exchanged sly glances. Babs once told me how her mother left her purse lying around.

'I'd better go,' Paula's hand was on the door. 'We'll hold our next meeting tomorrow.'

Babs asked, 'What time?'

'Is three o'clock okay? Sarah and I should have our ponies exercised by then.'

In bed that night, I hardly slept. In preparation for the meeting tomorrow I had written out little name cards:

President: Paula
Vice President: Sarah
Secretary: Babs
Treasurer: Katie

And the Pony Club forms were all filled in and ready to be sent off.

'You'd better not ride in the field this morning.' Dad was just finishing off his breakfast. 'It rained very heavily last night and the ground is slippery and soft. I don't want you cutting up the field.'

'Dad, I was just going to tack up and Paula is coming over to ride. She'll have to go out the road on her own. Unless . . .' I took a deep breath, '. . . could I go with her? For a hack on the road with Bluebell?'

'That depends.' His eyes flickered to Mam, waiting for her to give clearance. At least he was willing to trust me to take care of myself and my pony.

'We'll see when Paula comes.' She fidgeted with the sugar bowl.

'Absolutely no problem.' Paula spoke in her grown-up reassuring way. 'The two ponies behaved very well hacking up and down to the riding-school. We'll be on quiet roads all the time. And, Sarah might need the practice for her Road Safety Test. She'll probably have to do that when she's in the Pony Club.'

She had persuaded Mam, who was nodding, teapot in hand. 'I'm happier when you're both together, Paula. You know what Sarah is like. A car could be right up on her and she'd have her head in the clouds, oblivious!'

'I don't, Mam.' Not too loud. Don't get into a fight with her at this point.

'I'll keep an eye on her,' said Paula teasingly.

We trotted away and kept to the left side of the road. White fluffy clouds blew across the blue sunny sky and a fresh morning breeze rippled through the ponies' manes and tails as we trotted energetically up the hill.

Through the hedge we caught a glimpse of Babs and Katie in Clinton's field. Paula signalled to me and we started talking real loud and our voices rose above the clatter of hooves, carrying to their ears the sense of adventure they could not be part of, so that they'd feel jealous.

They were just standing there looking straight at us. Pretending not to see them, we laughed at some joke and nudged our ponies on faster.

Two other riders came into view up ahead. It was Niall and Trevor. We waved, then laughed giddily when they were gone past. They were looking back at us and laughing too.

At the crossroads. Paula decided to go home by another route, just in case Blackie decided to bolt if she turned him back the way we had come. He had a habit of doing that, she explained.

I trotted back on my own, slowing down near Clinton's.

'Oh, hi!' Babs stopped the makeshift see-saw and her little brother fell off on his bum. There was no sign of Katie.

'I wanted to tell you, Babs. I've made these lovely club membership cards.'

The smile altered on Babs' face and hovered there.

'You'll see them at the meeting today. Come down early if you can.'

The smirk on her face grew. 'I can't go down. I'm not allowed.'

I said lightly, 'Then we'll have a meeting without you.'

Triumphantly she faced me. 'Katie can't come either.'

A mist rose in front of my eyes. I kicked Bluebell on with my heels, urging her forward to trample on Babs, who was now standing before me.

She quickly stepped aside. 'Mam won't let me.'

'You couldn't keep a secret. You just had to tell,' checking the reins angrily.

'I didn't. It was Katie, if you'd like to know. She told her mother, who rang your mother and my mother. And your mother said we didn't have to give Paula any money to go to Lourdes or any other moony trip either. So there!' She halted, afraid no longer, eyes gleaming dangerously. 'She's not poor, is she, or what?'

I lifted the whip and she backed off again. 'She's not. She doesn't like asking for money. And anyway, her Mam is getting a fortune from Australia, because she owns a share in a mine there, the biggest in the world, and the Government are going to buy it off her. She doesn't need any money, now, does she?'

I brought the whip down on Bluebell and she bounded on to the road again.

Mam was sitting outside on a deck-chair. I threw myself down beside her, almost upending her.

'You didn't tell me about the club.'

'Mam, I don't have to tell you every little thing I do, do I? Babs just wanted to be leader, that's all.'

'The phone is ringing.' She pulled the sun-hat over her eyes again.

It was Paula. The friend with the polo ponies had offered her a job exercising them. It was boring kind of work, having to take them round and round in a circle for hours. But with the money, she could go to Pony Camp.

'That's great, Paula. I'll get Mam to post our entry forms right away.'

Still, I couldn't help feeling a tiny bit disappointed about our club.

11 PONY CAMP

It was not the usual summer, damp and green. The driest summer in a hundred years, the weathermen said. From high in the sky the midday sun shot down its long burning rays on the hillside and into the valley, lighting up withered fields of stubble, parched trees and hedges. Over in the paddock, wispy blades of yellow grass and buttercups poked thin and brittle out of cracked, sour-smelling earth. Red Admirals clustered brightly on the walls of the house. And rats. Rats everywhere, breeding fast and biting people.

Paula usually comes to my house after riding and we let the two ponies out in the field together while we cool off in my bedroom drinking diluted juice – when there is any – and reading pony books. Paula likes all things connected with horses.

The walls of my bedroom are covered with pony things, Bluebell's rosettes – two reds, a purple and a white – hang over the bed alongside a pony calendar, pony-club events' programmes, a print of an American Apaloosa horse my cousin sent from New Jersey, a small horseshoe, a postcard of a Connemara pony another cousin sent me from the Gaeltacht, and the African beating a drum – I can't bear to remove him yet. These are arranged in patterns, and decorated with bits of hair-slides and brooches.

'I didn't say it was definite. I said I *might* be able to go to Pony Camp with you!' Paula's body was tense, all wired up.

'You did say you would!'

This day had not gone well. Blackie and Bluebell nipped

at each other on the hack. On arriving home, dusty and weary, we had to water them, hauling bucketfuls up the slope to the trough. Then Mam bundled us into the fruit garden where zillions of gooseberries were waiting to be picked off bushes stitched into the long grass, their sharp thorns ready.

Afterwards we bathed our sore fingers. We were just beginning to cool off when Paula dropped her bombshell.

I opened the windows and flies flew in. I closed it – and we went on perspiring. 'You said you would,' I repeated, giving full attention to the thorn in my little finger. Pony Camp would be no fun without her. 'You said you would be able to get the money.' I felt let down. As if Paula was only pretending to be my friend when all along she didn't care. Just like the others.

'I thought Mum's friend was going to pay me for exercising her ponies,' her voice was low.

'She did promise, didn't she?' I challenged.

'What she gave me was the Pony Club subscription fee. I still haven't got the money for Camp. Now she doesn't need me. I think she has no money.' Paula's forehead was knotted in bumps and twists.

'It doesn't matter.' I gave up and wandered out into the kitchen.

Mam was sitting at the oval table, topping and tailing gooseberries, her fingers smudged with green. 'I forgot to tell you – Mrs Dealy from Pony Camp rang. She needs to know if you are going. She can arrange a box to collect Bluebell, and Blackie too if Paula wants. All ponies may stay at her farm for the week.' Scooping gooseberries on to the weighing scales. 'Well, what do you think?'

Idly sifting through the tops and tails with my index finger. 'I don't know. Bluebell mightn't like it there . . . other ponies might be kicking her.'

Mam was concentrating on the scales, 'That's three kilos!' Satisfaction sounded in her voice. 'Bluebell will be in a paddock with other ponies and will be quite comfortable. Mrs Dealy has assured me of that. And to avoid injury, the farrier will remove the ponies' back shoes.' She lifted her head and looked at me, eyes soft and wondering. 'What's the matter, Sarah? You were very keen on going. You still want to get on the School Cross-Country Team, don't you?'

Patterns were appearing in the heads and tails. 'I'd like Paula to come with me.'

Mam was working rhythmically again, adding to the little pile. 'There will be others at the camp, you know. I've no doubt you will make friends there. And it would be good experience for Bluebell. But it's your decision.'

The pattern became fixed. Bluebell jumping barrel height, showing the others what she could do. Maybe Mam was right. She needed the experience and I could not deprive her of it. This was something I had been looking forward to for a long time. With Paula of course, but . . .

Scatter the tops and tails in one quick movement. 'I've made up my mind, Mam. I'll go. You and Dad can have all the money in my post-office account to pay for it.'

'You pay half.' Mam gave me a quick kiss. Her cheek felt cool. 'The other half will be a present from Dad and me.'

'I'd better tell Paula.'

She was getting ready to leave. She listened, then hurried out past me, a determined look on her face. 'Maybe I could go as a working pupil. Seeing as Mrs M is one of the instructors, maybe I could ask her. But I'll have to check with Mum.'

She pedalled away and in no time she was on the 'phone, breathless. 'It's okay. I'm going. Mrs M said they would be glad of someone "capable" like me to help out.'

The sweet smell of jam cooking was wafting through the house. 'Great! We'll have mad crack!' And even though we giggled together about the 'someone capable' bit, it was true. They could not have a better assistant than Paula.

'I can take Blackie and I'll be able to sit in on some of the lectures too. Oh, and Mrs M says she'll take us to the pony rally tomorrow evening.'

'What's that for?' I asked.

'It's mainly to get us to meet the other people going to camp and our instructors. I have to go now. G'day, mate,' she mimicked.

We were off giggling again. Pony Camp was going to be great fun after all.

'She's turning into a jolly little mare,' Mrs M hadn't seen Bluebell for a while and she looked approvingly as I led her up the ramp. She settled her into her place beside Blackie.

'What did you bring?' Paula fastened her rope to the ring.

'Bucket, brush, and a small bag of oats. Tie it tight.'

'Same here.' She carefully knotted the rope.

'Ready, gels?' called Mrs M.

We jumped into the Range Rover beside her and, to loud whinnies from Bluebell, set off down the road. We were all in mighty humour and when Paula said, 'I think I'm going to burst,' our giggles nearly drowned out another huge whinny from Bluebell. Mrs M told us a story about a lovely mare she once had called Dawn Mist who could open any rope knot she set her mind to.

Just outside the village of Kildram we turned up a laneway and drove through a very wide gateway into a big farmyard. Mam's friend, Mrs Dealy, directed us to a parking spot alongside the wall of the hayshed. Riders and their ponies were grouped together on the other side of the yard. No one either of us recognised. I was glad Paula was with me.

'What do we do now?'

'Follow the others, I guess.'

We checked the girths and trotted over to join the group, already making its way down to the paddock. A big woman

in jodhpurs, fat-bottomed from sitting too long in the saddle, introduced herself. She read out three lists of names from her notebook and pointed to the three separate arenas. She came over to us and introduced herself. 'Hello, I'm Jill Horseman. Can you trot? Can you canter?' She stopped. 'Don't let them do that!' The sharpness of her tone caused Bluebell to jerk her head.

'Bluebell likes Blackie to lick her,' I explained, patting her, quieting her down.

'Oh, that's awfully nice.' She examined Bluebell's mouth, then Blackie's. 'Jolly good. Come with me.'

She opened the gate for us – into the smallest ring. We were in with the youngest group. With the babies!

Full of shock and disbelief, we stared in horror at each other.

On the way home, I could feel Paula ready to explode, this time with rage. I was right!

As the horsebox drove away from our gateway she burst out angrily, 'Imagine being told how to mount! What does she think we are? Beginners? In that tiny little paddock, we won't get a chance to do any jumping!'

I nodded dumbly. The instructor had said Bluebell was two years old. That was all she knew!

'Don't worry,' Mam consoled us as she stirred the big saucepan of jam. 'You'll be moved up to the next group when the instructress sees what you are able to do.'

We had to be at the camp at 9 am next morning. I was waiting with Paula who was queueing with Blackie for the farrier when Jill Horseman called me over.

'Sarah, you will be joining the Intermediate group today.'

I hesitated. 'What about Paula?'

'Paula and Blackie are in Group 1 for the moment.' She strode off.

Paula was still in the beginners' group! It was clear from her white face that she had heard. But there was no time to talk because Jill was giving instructions.

'Everyone, oil your pony's hooves. Now.'

Hoof oil? We looked at one another.

A girl in the queue behind us said, 'You can use mine.' I recognised Pam, the girl we had met at Kill show who had offered to plait Bluebell.

'Thanks,' I took it from her. 'Bluebell's probably don't need oil.' But I oiled them anyway.

Paula oiled Blackie's hooves too.

Jill was telling us to mount up and I joined my new group. I almost wished I was still in with the babies so that I could be with Paula.

'Sarah, please don't hold up the ride!'

I went into the ring full of foreboding, feeling Bluebell tense and nervous under me, and I guessed there would be trouble. Sure enough! Bluebell began to act up straightway. She was lonely for Blackie and wary of all the strange ponies. She refused to move freely and when she spotted Blackie in the other ring, she whinnied loudly in his direction.

'Hurry up, Sarah. We haven't got all day. David, heels down. Sit up straight. Sarah, kick her on!'

It was hard work trying to keep up as we went round and round and my face grew hotter under the tight helmet. Clouds of dust from the ponies' hooves funnelled into our noses and mouths. My eyes hurt and my clothes were sticking to my body. Sweat was dripping off Bluebell.

'Dismount!'

We all got off and after walking our ponies back into the yard to water them, then queued at the tap to douse our faces and rub away the streaks of mud. In the barn I removed Bluebell's saddle and bridle and tethered her in the row with the others. Then I took out my lunch-box and sat on a bale a little distance away. Other riders were sitting together in a group.

'Hi!' Paula threw herself on a bale beside me, and removed her helmet to show a line of sweat on her brow. 'I had to help the younger ones with their tack and watering.'

'How did it go?' Too tired to eat, I closed my lunch-box and drank my juice instead.

She made a face without saying anything. We rested, watching the group of older girls and boys from the Advanced group chatting and laughing together. 'That's John.' Paula nudged me, directing her gaze at a short, heavy-looking boy. 'His pony has a saddle sore. He just presses, to make him buck. For a laugh.'

One of the group was getting up, coming over to us. It was Pam. 'Hi,' she said. 'I wonder could I borrow your bucket, Sarah?'

'Sure.' I got up, took my red plastic bucket and filled it at the tap, then carried into her pony in the barn. Together we watched him drinking.

'He's beautiful,' I said. 'Is he graded?'

'Yes. He's Grade B.'

'Only Grade B!' Afterwards Paula was amazed, then she added, 'I like Pam. She's not a boast like the others.'

'What does it mean, to say your pony is Grade B?' I remembered Niall talking about grades, but I'd forgotten what he said.

'It means he has won a lot of points and is eligible to jump in Grade B competitions. She probably went to shows all over the country to qualify. You win points every time you're placed in a competition. Grade A is the highest standard, needing the highest number of points.'

'What grade would our ponies be?'

'Grade D.' Her forehead twitched, showing a thin worry line. 'We can only go upwards.'

The group was stirring and wearily we got up off the bales. Our veterinary lecture was about to start.

Paula was allowed to join our group for Mr Maxwell's talk and we sat together in the shade of the barn, listening and taking notes.

Outside again, another girl, who was not on our ride, asked if she could borrow my bucket.

'Sure. Take it whenever you want, only leave it back.'

'Thanks.' She stopped, then looked at me closely and said, 'My name is Claire. Didn't we both have a joint lesson once with Mrs M at the riding-school? You were on a little grey.'

The girl who couldn't tie her saddle!

'Oh, hi,' I wasn't sure what else to say.

'Do you like your pony?' she gave me a quick glance.

'Oh, yes,' I said shyly. 'She's really wonderful.'

Her own tone was quiet and low as if afraid someone might hear her. 'I hate mine. Most times I get up he starts bucking and I end up on the ground. I broke my collar-bone again last month. I liked my last pony better. But this one wins loads of competitions. This year we'll probably go to the Dublin Horse Show.' She went off with the bucket.

At least, I didn't have that problem. It was a struggle to get Bluebell even to walk into the ring for dressage. And for the rest of the lesson we trailed at the end of the ride.

When it was time to go home I couldn't see Paula and guessed she had left early. Bluebell was spending the night with the other mares. As Dad drove into the yard, a loud piercing whinny came from the paddock and she put her head over the gate as we passed.

'Maybe I should check if she's all right.' I glanced at Dad.

'Don't worry, she'll be fine.' He patted my knee.

When we got home, Mam opened her eyes wide in astonishment. 'Lord, Sarah, you must have been rolling in that dust!' She quickly disappeared to run the bath. Afterwards, I still couldn't eat with the pain in my tummy, so I went straight to bed.

'I'll leave out a shirt and sweater for you for the morning. Coats should not be worn in this kind of heat.' Mam came in and made a bundle of my clothes for the washing-machine.

'Mam!' I sat up in bed. 'I must wear a jacket! I can't be different from everyone else. I'd be the joke of the Camp! And I'm supposed to have a hairnet for tomorrow. Jill Horseman said we all have to wear one.'

'I don't care what Jill Horseman said.' Mam spoke through gritted teeth.

In the morning, there was a phone call from Paula to say she wasn't going to Camp because she had to baby-sit her brother.

My back felt tired. Dad drove me over on his way to work. As we pulled into the yard, my eyes fearfully roamed the paddock, checking to see if Bluebell was among the other ponies and if she was all right.

She was on her own and she trotted over, ears cocked eagerly and when I gave her some oats, she gobbled enthusiastically. I tacked her up, pleased that she seemed livelier.

But during the lesson she behaved worse than before. She seemed to have made enemies among the bigger ponies and when we came near, they put back their ears and tried to kick her.

At the mid-morning break, after Mrs Dealy had given us all some strawberries and cream, I brought more oats to Bluebell in the barn.

'This might perk you up.' She thrust her head into the bucket. 'You'll get more later on if you behave.' I pushed her soft muzzle away and reached for the bridle to slip it on her.

John's black pony was tethered alongside her. Without warning, he lashed out, kicking her in the belly. With a squeal of pain, Bluebell moved away but another pony connected with her.

Her ears suddenly went back and she kicked out at them. But it was no use. She was hemmed in on both sides. They were thumping her as if she were a drum.

Untie her headcollar fast. I've got to get her out. The drumming grew louder in its rhythm.

'Hold on.' Miranda from the Advanced group appeared at my side. She stretched in to catch the black pony by the headcollar and moved him away.

'Are you all right?' Leading out Bluebell, she helped me saddle up, waiting in silence until my hands had stopped shaking. She said severely, 'Don't you know you're not to feed your pony when there are other ponies nearby?' She went back to her friends, and as I moved about Bluebell checking her for cuts and bruises, I could hear them laughing. Miraculously, Bluebell was not hurt. My own legs ached from her hooves, and later they showed up black and blue.

Outside, Jill Horseman was giving instructions to tack up. 'Hurry on, Sarah,' she called. 'We haven't got all day.'

'You're okay now, Bluebell,' I whispered as I mounted, trying to reassure her. 'You're okay.' But I knew that after

her experience there was no way she was going to settle for the rest of the ride.

Swopping ponies was part of the next lesson. The heavy boy, John, exchanged with me. His pony moved freely enough but I couldn't concentrate on my own riding, watching him tugging and sawing at Bluebell's reins. She gave a small rear.

'John, don't yank her like that.' Jill roared at him. 'That's a lovely quiet pony, a beautiful temperament. You don't treat her like an old nag.'

His face flushed under his cap and his ears turned the colour of ripe plums. He didn't try any tricks again, even when she refused to canter for him. Changing back to our own ponies, he threw her reins at me.

'Ride on!' Jill was shouting again.

Despite every effort, squeezing with my legs, digging in my heels, pushing with my seat, Bluebell was slowing down, Then, taking a step backwards, she daintily folded her hind legs and sat down in the ring.

'Get up, Bluebell. I'm not getting off,' kicking her sides. Everyone laughed their heads off at us, even people in the other rings. After getting a clip of the whip she staggered to her feet again and shook herself, showering Jill Horseman in dust.

At lunch break I watered Bluebell while the rest of the group were eating and I gave a bucket to the two ponies on each side of her as well. Going back and forth was hazardous. You were in danger of tripping over bags of equipment, cylinders of fly-repellent, jars of hoof oil, sacks of bran and mash and nuts as well as cod-liver oil tablets. But my old bucket was most useful.

Back resting on my bale, I waited for the call to mount up again.

Jill Horseman was having a word with the rest of the group. When she saw me she came over. 'Would you like to talk to that girl Louise? She's rather shy.' I glanced at a girl sitting on her own. 'No problem!' quickly getting to my feet. 'But first I have to give Bluebell some more water.'

Her face softened in a smile. 'I heard what happened with your pony. I hope she isn't too upset.'

Louise had disappeared into the barn ahead of me. Inside she was feeding bits of a sandwich to her pony. The pony had a soft muzzle like Bluebell's and I rubbed it gently.

'What his name?'

'Flicker. He's my best friend.' She patted him hard.

'Where do you live?' I asked.

'Aille.'

'That's near where I live!'

'Well, I go to school in Dublin, so I don't have any friends around.'

We tacked up together and then walked our ponies out into the sunshine, heading across the yard to the rings. Half way across, Bluebell quickened her pace. Cocking her ears, she veered off towards the main exit.

'Back, Bluebell, back!' With difficulty, shoulder to her flank, I managed to force her back.

In the ring I had to push, push all the time to keep her going, but her movements got slower and slower until finally she sat down again.

'Dismount!' Jill Horseman shouted. 'That will be all for today!'

Bluebell hurried, pushing me towards the exit gate.

After I set her loose in the paddock with the other mares, her sad look and high anxious whinny followed me out into the yard.

The lesson in the jumping arena promised to be the toughest of all, with fences more difficult than Bluebell had attempted before. But I was prepared for the worst.

'I'm not hungry, where's my body protector?' Trying to get past.

Mam's arms flopped helplessly by her side and she joined in the search. 'Here,' handing me the blue padded jacket, helping to put it on.

'Thanks. I'll probably roll off a few times. I don't mind about myself. It's Bluebell I'm worried about. She's only a youngster.'

Mam sighed and held out my lunch-box. 'I wish you weren't taking all this so seriously. After all, it was meant to be a bit of fun . . . Remember, Bluebell has some experience of going around a course so it won't be totally new to her. It will probably be better than you think.'

Of course, Mam was dead wrong. The type of fences used for the jumping were all new to Bluebell. And scary. At the third fence, a wall, she refused. Again and again I put her at it until she performed her trick of sitting down in front of it. Pam was one of the riders with a clear round and John ended on the ground after a tumble. It was the end of his riding. Jill found out about the saddle sore and grounded him.

Later, as I was leading Bluebell across the yard, she took a quick swing over to the horse-box and had her feet on the loading ramp before I could stop her, looking pleadingly at me with her two funny eyes but I yanked her away. In the barn, I put my arms around her neck to comfort her. 'Only one more day, Bluebell. That's all.'

The day of my D-Test, jumping competition and Dressage Test!

Sitting up in bed that night, I took out the pony manual. I still had to learn the different parts of the horse and tack for my D-Test. Suddenly everything went black.

'Aw, Mam! How am I going to know this and get Bluebell to go for me tomorrow?'

From the doorway, Mam sounded disgusted. 'Give her a few whacks of the whip. She's playing up on you. That should wake her up. Leave that light off and go to sleep.'

My voice rose hoarsely. 'You're not allowed use the whip in dressage. And you should have bought me new jodhpurs. Everyone is laughing at those yellow ones. Couldn't you get to the shop in the morning? Mam, why won't you answer me!' The door closed behind her.

Next morning, we were late, my jodhpurs having ripped again.

But when I went to tack up, I noticed that a few other ponies were still tethered in the barn, including Claire's.

'What's up?' I asked Louise, who was plaiting her pony while studying the movements for her Dressage Test from a sheet stuck to the wall.

'They've gone lame.' Louise put her leg in the stirrup and hoisted herself into the saddle. 'They can't be ridden.'

Wishing her luck I grabbed the comb and plaiting bands. It would soon be my turn.

Jill Horseman bent down and examined Bluebell's hooves, then straightened up, nodding in approval.

'They're good and hard. She's a fine healthy pony; obviously you keep her in healthy conditions. Can I take you for your D-Test now? The others completed theirs earlier this morning.'

She led the way down to a shaded corner of the field. First she got me to walk, trot and canter, clockwise and anti-clockwise. It was very hard work getting Bluebell into canter and keeping her there. Then I had to halt and dismount correctly. She asked me, 'What type of a bit do you have?'

'An egg-butt snaffle.' It was lucky I had looked that up last night.

'Right . . . What type of a nose-band do you have?'

'A cavesson nose-band.'

'Right. Okay, parts of the pony. What's that?' She pointed to the horse's lower joint.

'The ankle, I mean, the fetlock.' I remembered this from our veterinary lecture.

'Last question: How often are you supposed to worm your pony?'

'About every season.' I wasn't going to forget that, was I?

'Well, you're the first person to answer that question correctly today. By the way, do you know your Dressage Test?'

'Not very well.' Even after hours of poring over the sheet telling me things like Enter at A in working trot, X halt, Salute, Proceed at working trot, C track left. How was I supposed to know what all those letters meant?

She went on to explain that points on the outside of the arena were marked by different letters, apart from X which was the dead centre of the arena. These letters were there to tell me exactly where to circle, where to go from walk to trot, or trot to canter and back. That was as much as I had to understand for my level. She gave me a tip for memorising these outer letters in order: 'All King Edward's Horses Carry Many Bloody Fools.'

But today, the movements at points AKEHCMBF

wouldn't have to be memorised. She wrote our names on the test sheet, then pointed to my leathers and told me to oil them while I waited.

I mounted very carefully and did a beautiful canter ahead of her up towards the gate. She laughed. 'Well able to canter when she wants to!'

Strangely enough, I felt more confident than I had all week. Wanting to make sure that I didn't have the same trouble cantering in the Dressage arena as I had for my D-Test, I went on a gallop down to the bottom of the field to waken Bluebell up, and while I waited for my turn, I studied the other riders going before me. Louise did a perfect show. Then the judge leaned out of the car parked at the end of the arena and called, 'Sarah Quinn on Bluebell.'

They beeped the horn and Bluebell spooked, but I quickly circled and urged her to a nice trot before entering at A.

Jill Horseman read out instructions for me in a loud clear voice. Having studied the others was a help. It all went so quickly for so much worry and preparation. Bluebell had gone very well except she broke too early from canter into trot.

Now it was time for the jumping competition. Bluebell went slowly into the first fence. I leaned forward. 'Go on, Bluebell. Remember, you're going home today.' As if she knew what I was saying, her ears twiddled and she cleared the fence at a trot, going on to the other fences in the same way. Coming up to the wall, I took one hand off the reins and gave her a good slap in case she was thinking of refusing. She knocked the last pole, but I didn't mind. At least she hadn't refused.

That evening, the Pony Club chairman awarded certificates to everyone who passed. I got a D-Test certificate, along with a special rosette for hard work. Louise got a special rosette too for the most improved pony. Later, having led Bluebell into the paddock, I went to check if Louise was going to the club disco. She saw me and yelled something.

Robert was walking towards me carrying a bucket. With a big grin, he sloshed the water all over me.

When the parents arrived for the barbecue we were sopping wet. But we weren't cold and no one needed a clothes change. We had a great time dancing to disco music in the barn and eating chips and burgers.

But Bluebell was impatient to get away, and while Louise and I were swopping telephone numbers at the ramp, she walked into the horsebox herself.

Back in her field, she lay down in the grass for a nice long roll, hiding herself in a cloud of dust. Bono swished his tail around her, giving out welcoming barks in between the sneezes.

Next day, when I woke, my D-Test certificate looked down at me from my bedroom wall, and it was lunchtime.

Bluebell was still lying in the grass, exhausted from her week of hard work away from home. Bending down to pat her, she cocked one ear to listen. 'Other ponies won't be able to bully you next time.'

Next time, she would know better how to defend herself. And I would know better how to take care of her, I promised.

Paula was very interested in what I had learned in Dressage and I gave her a two-legged 'demo'.

It occurred to me, guiltily, that I hadn't missed her too much after all.

Up and over. Come on, Bluebell, fifty more jumps to go. Mile after mile they stretch out in front, blue and white, yellow and black, and an enormous wall dominating the horizon. But Bluebell is getting tired. She is barely rising to the fences. Now into that bank and as we launch up there is a glimpse of a huge drain. She somersaults!

Aagh! It was a surprisingly soft landing. Hardly daring to, I sat up and looked around to find myself sitting on the floor, safely wrapped in the soft duvet and the 'phone ringing in the distance.

Mam was at the door. 'What are you doing? Paula is on the 'phone.'

Groaning. Riding was the last thing I wanted to do. And Bluebell probably felt the same. I hurried out.

Her voice sounded thin. 'I won't be able to go riding with you for a few days.'

'That's okay.' Breathe freely again. 'Will you be coming over anyway?'

'I can't. I'm going on holidays to my uncle in Kildare and we're leaving today. I wish we could take Blackie too.'

'I'll ring on Sunday to see if you're back.'

'Leave it until late.'

When the dew lifted, I lay on the sun-bed outside the back door and, surrounded by the smells of summer, relaxed in the warmth. Bluebell would be happy to have the week off; she too needed a long rest. I wanted time to find my land legs again. They seemed to be going bandy. I didn't want legs like Mrs M or Mr Boylan – he walked as if a horse was still underneath him.

'Sarah, will you help pick the peas?' Mam was peering at me, saucepan in hand.

'Do I have to? Okay.'

Actually I enjoy picking – and eating – peas, when seated comfortably on a bucket surrounded by soft greenery.

Loud jangling was followed by a flutter of brightly coloured print at the ditch.

'Hi!' It was Babs.

She slid down into the pea patch. I hadn't seen much of her during the summer and I wasn't sure that I wanted to see her now. She had a pleased look about her, like a dog with another dog's bone. She was wearing a new yellow dress, new runners that didn't match and a big charm bracelet.

'I was in Paris,' she said, swaying from the waist, hands behind her back, voice boastful. 'When I was on the underground train, I had to sit beside a Frenchman.'

For some reason, Mam found this wildly funny and fell off the rickety crate laughing. Babs grinned widely, eyes flashing, basking in the attention.

'Where's Katie?' I had to ask.

'On holidays in the Canaries.' Babs hummed while she ate. 'Where's Paula?'

'On holidays.'

Babs couldn't hide her pleased look and she ate some more. 'Do you have to ride Bluebell today?'

'No. She's resting after Pony Camp.'

Our eyes met in a sidelong glance and I knew we were going to have a good day. Babs was in a fun mood.

Mam brought out some cool drinks and urged us to hurry and fill the basin because it was going to rain. Frowning up at the clouds in the sky with the warning, 'Wet vegetables don't keep.'

When she was gone out of earshot, Babs said carefully, 'Will we eat these?' green eyes fixed on the peas already picked.

'I don't mind.' We filled our pockets and sat on the ditch munching in a relaxed state.

'I think I feel a drop of rain,' Babs was patting her head and looking gravely at her palm. 'Come up to the ranch house.'

I was going to say why couldn't we go to her house, that I'd never been inside her house, but thought it better not get her into a bad mood.

'Don't let them see you,' Babs pulled me down below the fence. 'If Mam knows I'm here, she'll make me mind the baby. Let's put a proper roof on the ranch house.'

It was dark when I got home. Heavy clouds had gathered in the deep dark sky, bringing the night in earlier.

'I can't believe it's so late.' Bang the door shut, heaving for breath. Wait for it. Dad and Mam were sitting on the

couch together and they stared at me in silence. I said,
'Babs codded me about the time and she wouldn't let me go
home even though I wanted to.'

'Did you ask Mrs Tipping?' Mam got up looking cross.

'She wasn't there.'

Mam was still annoyed. 'You'd better get out there in the
morning and finish those peas.'

All night long, the rain fell in torrents, dashing over the gut-
ters and drumming in the buckets. In the morning
Bluebell's trough was overflowing and water was streaming
down the driveway. But Dad warned that we would need a
week of rain to get our water supply back to normal. It
rained all next day too. From the study window, I could see
Bluebell sheltering under the big ivy-covered tree. The grass
had darkened and the birds were singing with joy.

Smell of roses and weeds and damp mint, as well as the
sound of dripping leaves, as I made my way over to Babs'
house, the ground still wet after the rain, the mist resting
over the valley. She waved from her window and came running out. As the dog chased the rabbits from the banks, we
searched for mushrooms in the wet grass.

I showed Babs a trick Dad had shown me, how to string
mushrooms on a *trawneen*. At the ranch house, she pro-
duced a box of matches and old newspaper. We made a
heap of old dead wood and leaves and fir branches and
started a fire. After a lot of smoke it burned warmly. We put
the mushrooms into a foil tin on top of the fire. Delicious!

'Where were you all day?' Mam looked vicious. But I was in
no mood for her.

'You're always giving out! You're always in a bad
humour!'

She calmed down when I tossed her the mushrooms I'd
saved. 'Have something to eat . . . Oh, I nearly forgot.
Paula was here. She left you a present.'

I opened up the parcel to find a plaster model of a Connemara pony. I put it on my window-sill where even people passing by outside might see it, and rang her. 'It's beautiful, Paula. You shouldn't have. I know it must have cost you a lot of money. Will you be riding tomorrow?'

'No, I can't. Mum is taking me to town to get a new school skirt.'

I put the 'phone down. The end of the holidays. That was what had spoiled the day, the thought that the summer holidays were nearing an end. Soon a whole new school term would begin.

A feeling crept into my stomach. Like a log in the canal water, at first barely recognisable, then becoming more familiar, like the face of a crocodile. An old feeling I hadn't got for a long time.

There was another feeling lurking under the surface. A feeling that now things might be different. Before, when Babs was my best friend, if I fought with her I had no one until I made it up with her again.

Now, I thought, I have Paula.

12 THE CANAL

We lined up in the school yard, hoping to see our new teacher. Babs, poking and pushing, was already up to her old tricks, even though it was only first day back. Winking at me, she said loudly to Katie, 'Your socks are lovely.' Then turning back to me, 'Aren't her socks awful?' sniggering loudly.

Everyone liked our new teacher, Mrs Pyne. She waved her arms about and spoke about honour and being able to trust us. No one was sure what she meant.

There was just one big problem. She gave a lot of homework. Well, she didn't exactly *give* it. She told us we could decide ourselves how much we wanted to do – which meant you really had to do it all. And with the evenings getting shorter, there wasn't much time to fit in all this homework and the riding.

We jogged into the countryside, past glistening hedges of blackberries, reddened haws and rosehips. The ponies' rhythm drove away all wandering thoughts of school, lines, homework and teachers and sent them floating off on the soft west wind that blew in our faces. A swift surge of energy matched the strong movement of my pony beneath me.

Bluebell sneaked out in front, and put on a spurt every time Blackie went to pass her. We turned left towards Oughterard, and at the top of Sheeogue Hill, we slowed to a walk. No point in tiring them just yet.

Relaxing now, leaning back, one hand on Bluebell's rump. 'Dad says that in order to get a loan for our stud farm, we would have to give the bank manager some "cholesterol" or something and that the banks didn't fancy horsy people as customers.'

Paula was leaning back too, tanned face smooth in the evening sun. 'My Mum says I'd better marry a millionaire, speaking of which . . .' she made a face.

A figure on horseback was gaining on us. I wondered if it was Trevor and my heart beat faster. He waved.

'It's Niall.' Paula shortened her reins. I wasn't mad about him joining us either. Paula and I had lots of secrets to tell each other. It was not the same with a boy around.

'Whoa, Teabag.' Drawing level, grinning under the tight cap. 'Is it okay if I ride with you?' Already his pony had fallen into stride.

I looked questioningly at Paula who nodded. Teabag bared his teeth at Blackie so we moved quickly into a trot again.

We had reached the end of the demesne wall when Bluebell suddenly stopped. Nervously she watched the sheep bobbing and biting at the ivy. I steadied her, calmly nudging her over for a close look. After a few seconds she lifted her head and whinnied to them in welcome.

'Amazing!' Niall rode up alongside.

'Yeah . . . When Grandad first saw her she was lying in a field, with bullocks and heifers all around her. They were the best of friends. But she's probably never seen sheep before.'

Ahead, Paula was slowing down, waiting for us. Through the trees we could see the ruins of Oughterard Abbey.

'That's where old Mr Guinness is buried,' said Niall.

Paula raised her eyes to heaven. 'We know,' she answered. 'We're going in there.' She led the way, opening the gate, and we turned up the tree-lined path to the graveyard, the sound of the ponies' hooves deadened by the fallen beech leaves.

'Do you like Guinness?' asked Niall.

'No, I hate it.' Paula gave a mock shudder.

'My dad blurps when he drinks it.' Niall gave such a long loud belch to show us what he meant that even Paula had to laugh.

We tethered our ponies and slipped through the stile, clambering down among the tombstones. We sat on a sloping slab for a rest, keeping watch on our grazing ponies outside and gazing out over the sunny, empty fields. We didn't talk much. Paula and I had brought apples and we ate them.

Niall went over to have a look and came back. 'It says Mr Guinness died in . . . '

'Oh, Niall, you're able to read.' Paula laughingly offered him a bite of her Granny Smith.'

Back on our ponies, we rode down towards the canal, then walked in single file along the tow-path, deep water on our left, and reached the lock where the boats were moored.

'See, this is where the clay bank slipped away.' Where

Paula was pointing, a section of the earthen mound had collapsed into the canal. 'The rain must have caused it.'

'Bluebell had better go in front.' I kicked her on. 'She's part Connemara and very sure-footed.'

With Bluebell in front, our pace slowed down, her attention fixed on every new sight and sound. But when Teabag went to edge out in front, Blackie nipped him. Two swans hissed at us from the water and spread their wings, making such a noise that Bluebell whinnied in alarm.

'This is the place,' said Paula.

We inspected the ditch surrounding the field of stubble, where it was low and muddy with hoofmarks. So this was the jump Paula had been talking about.

'Want to try Teabag at it?' Paula politely offered Niall first go.

'I reckon so.' Niall quickly collected his reins. 'Teabag is great at doing ditches. On the junior hunt we jumped loads of these. But if you like, you can go first.'

Paula nodded. Blackie swept over it without any trouble and Teabag followed. But Bluebell didn't like the look of it. She walked forward, stretched her head and neck out over it and stopped. She wouldn't budge. While the others jumped back and over, I spoke quietly to her, trying to build up her confidence in an effort to get her over it.

'Why won't she jump?' Niall reined in beside us.

He must not be allowed to think that she was no use. 'She's very young,' I explained. 'She has absolutely no experience of ditches. There are none in Galway, only stone walls. If it was a stone wall, she'd fly over it.'

I pressed her on again. But Bluebell was distracted by a movement up at the lock. Loud whoops and shouts and the sound of splashing hooves burst over the water.

'Oh great!' said Niall sarcastically. 'It's Peter Orum and his friend. I think they've seen us!' He manoeuvred his pony a little away from us.

They came thundering down the path towards us, whips

flying, standing up in the saddles like cowboys, jackets flapping in the wind as they shouted and yelled.

We drew back to let them pass, but they were slowing down. Peter's chestnut and his friend's strong cob were lathered with sweat. I recognised the friend. It was John from Pony Camp. I wondered if his pony still had that saddle sore.

'Having problems?' Peter was looking at me and Paula, slapping his whip against his boot. Then he edged his pony in beside us, jostling Bluebell. Before I realised his intention, he brought his whip down across her hind quarters. She bucked in fright, kicking out at the other pony, but I managed to stay on and tried to reverse out of the way. She was trembling and bunched up under me as if she were getting ready to bolt. And she kept on backing, backing across the narrow tow-path, towards the canal water. Frantically I kicked her to go forward.

Paula spotted the danger and got off. She walked slowly towards us, hand outstretched, ready to grab Bluebell's bridle. But Bluebell was too frightened. She wasn't listening to me. All I could do now was hang on, keep talking to her, even as her back legs began slipping and sliding, sliding down into the deep canal water.

Then, as if she suddenly became aware of the danger herself, her ears went forward and she stepped clear on to solid ground.

My heart was still thumping loudly when I faced Peter and John. 'I don't need to use brute force on my pony. She responds better to kindness and gentleness.' Despite my best efforts to steady it, my voice sounded peculiar.

For a moment, they were silent.

'Who'd sell anyone a pony like that?' said Peter looking serious.

'Who'd buy a pony like that!' said John. They began to laugh. They nearly fell off their ponies laughing. Then they swung about and slapping their ponies they galloped away towards the lock again. One of them shouted back, 'Coming, Niall? Or do you want to stay with the girls!' Roars of laughter again.

Niall's face was an angry red. Paula who had got back up on Blackie again, said, 'Peter isn't able to ride for nuts.' Her voice was cutting. 'His pony goes galloping up the road and he's not even able to control him. Come on, Sarah, forget about them. We'll try this ditch again.'

This time, Bluebell was in better humour for jumping. She took the lead from Blackie and Teabag, faltered forward and over the ditch. She had done it! Her first ditch. She was on her way to her first cross-country!

'Good girl!' I stroked and patted her, breathing deeply, big deep breaths that stopped the shaking.

I thought to myself that she must be the best pony in the whole world. And the most beautiful, with her cute little white face. 'She's good all right.' Niall leaned over in the saddle to pat her and I got off and picked some red clover for her. 'And you're getting two potatoes when we get home.'

'Look!' Paula was pointing up the path towards the lock. 'Peter's in the canal!'

John was running up and down the path and when he saw us approaching, he shouted, 'Save him!' Peter's frightened face was turned towards us, his bleached blond hair streaming in the water like seaweed, his pony beside him mashing reeds and water.

I climbed down off Bluebell and shouted to him, 'Let go of your reins.' I had never felt so calm in my life.

His pony struggled up on to the bank on his knees, saturated in mud and looking like a hippo. Reaching out I grabbed his bridle, and immediately he shook himself, slinging mud and water all over us.

'Here,' I thrust the reins at John, warning him to remove the saddle, that the pony would roll.

But he ignored the reins, pulling at my arm instead, his

face white. 'Don't mind the pony. What about Peter?'

'Shut up!' Niall caught him roughly by the shoulder and, pushing him aside, untied the pony's saddle himself.

'Help!' roared Peter.

Paula looked away.

'He won't drown.' Niall seemed in no hurry to rescue him either.

'Look,' I faced them both. 'There's no point in taking chances. The canal is full of treacherous currents. He could be dragged under.'

Niall said grumpily, 'What will we do? Jump in after him? No way! I've my good clothes on me.' His hands clutched at his denim jacket.

'No need,' I told him. 'Just give me your stirrup-leathers. Hurry.' Already I had the buckle on one of Peter's leathers open, freeing it from the saddle.

Niall was staring at me. It had suddenly dawned on him what I was going to do. 'We'll use Bluebell,' he said, and quickly set to work on his own leathers. Reluctantly Paula did the same.

We buckled all the leathers together, forming a long rope, and tied one end to Bluebell's girth. Below us, Peter clutched at the weeds, making spluttering, gurgling sounds.

I shouted to him to catch and he reached out, grabbing the stirrup at the other end of the rope. 'Now,' I told him, 'hold on. Don't let go!'

Catching hold of Bluebell's bridle, I led her forward. She pulled slightly, chewing on the bit, then pranced daintily forward and slowly she hauled Peter towards the bank. With a huge sucking sound, Peter's shoulder lifted out of the water. He stood there in the shallows, dripping with muck and greenery.

'The eejit!' Niall turned to us angrily. 'It wasn't deep at all.' He turned back to the figure climbing out of the water. 'You were sittin' down in it lettin' on to be drowned,' he accused him. 'I've a good mind to throw you in again.'

Peter came slowly up the bank, wiping his eyes and his nose. He smelled of stale fish and his crying made him look even worse.

'Stop crying,' John said contemptuously. 'You're saved!'

But Peter let out a wail. 'My boots are still in the water.' It was only then that we noticed he was in his socks. 'They got stuck in the mud,' he blubbered, 'and I was trying to find them. That's why I didn't want to come out. I can't go home without them. My mother is going to kill me. She's in a very bad humour,' sniffling, blowing green slime out of his nose.

'Why is she in a bad humour?' Paula seemed interested now.

'Dad is gone to England to get married.'

'He can't.' Niall sounded fed up. 'He is married to your mother.'

'He's going to get married again, to someone in a Registry Office.'

'Will you have two mothers then?' Niall asked him. This made Peter start crying again.

'Are they both invited to your Confirmation,' I asked.

'I suppose so.'

'You can't,' Paula objected. 'There won't be room.'

There was silence. Then Niall took off his jacket and handed it to Peter, saying, 'Look, there's no way we can get your boots out of the water when they are stuck in the bottom. It's lucky you're not stuck down there with them. Dead. Look, you'd better come to my house to dry out. My mother won't mind when it's not me.'

Patting Bluebell's face and smoothing her white blaze, I thought of the very clever part she had played in the rescue, and how, if I were to die or get drowned or anything, I'd want her to have a good home, like Paula's.

Essay competition: I head mine 'The Rescue.'

It was the bridle path to Galway, that lay, late in October, before the three riders whose story I am about to tell you.

They rode in single file along the left bank of the canal. She was in front, her figure muffled from the weather by a hooded cloak which covered herself and her pony.

On the pony behind her was a figure which looked like a girl of similar height and build, also wrapped from head to toe and sitting side-saddle.

As the sinking sun cast weak shadows on to the shrouded waters they were passing, its rays fell on the third traveller. He rode tall and straight, well wrapped like his companions, his wide-brimmed hat hiding his face and his long cloak dipping well down over his horse's flank. Despite the cloak and the dusk and the mud that clung to its limbs, the dying sun picked up the dull glint off his stallion's powerful neck, the sheen off its mane and quarters.

With nodding heads and swinging tails the horses laboured on, making only muffled sounds as they squashed their way through the soft mud. So far they were making good progress and hoped to join the western road at Enfield that would lead them away from their enemies . . .

'Sarah, come on. Everyone else is gone to gym for indoor hockey.'

'All right, Niall. Stop pulling at me.' Race to the hall, togging out in leggings and sweater, taking up position.

They kept up a good pace, the little dark grey pony with the white blaze eagerly leading the way, everyone's lives depending on her sureness of foot.

Now and then, the shafts of dim fire that leaped from the stallion's tail and mane were reflected on the surface of the dark slick water that lapped and gurgled below them on its winding passage through the reeds. It was a long way to Galway port. What hope had they of avoiding capture none of the three children dared to think . . .

Stick flashing past surprised faces, into the goal-mouth.

'Sarah!' Trevor's face was dark and angry. 'Can't you remember whose team you're on!'

Oh no! Not an own goal!

In the end, the essay did not turn out quite as well as I had expected. It got too long and I was worried that I wouldn't get it finished before our hallowe'en break. Still, when I showed it to teacher she asked me to read it for the class.

But it was Susan who got the highest marks. Susan!

'Yours should have got first,' Niall said when I sat down. 'It was miles better.' My old teacher always gave me first. Somehow I don't think I'm going to like this one as much.

I wondered why Niall was always so nice to me, when I hadn't been especially nice to him.

13 MISSING

When the wind blew, it was from the north. Under a pink sky, the landscape lay colourless, except for the green ivy that clung to bare trees and the dark sloes that glinted in the bushes. In the paddock Bluebell pawed white crystals of frost off the chilled grass, and in the garden it was time for pruning.

'The school riding-team is going to be selected at the junior Cross-Country Trials next month. I'm going, that is, if Blackie is fit enough.' Paula's fingers trawled her pony's mane. 'What about you?'

'Dad says I can!'

'Of course.' Paula, deliberately cool although her voice trembled a little, flicked her reins and the hair out of her eyes with the same movement. 'We'll have to build up the ponies' stamina so that we can keep going for miles.'

For ever. Bluebell stirred uneasily under the force of my ferocious pats.

Paula was looking at her watch. 'It's getting dark already. I'd better be going. See you at school tomorrow.'

'Hi!' Niall puffed past me in the gym hall, slowing down. 'I called but you had gone out riding. Going to the Cross-Country qualifier?'

'I think so.'

'Brilliant!' Chest heaving. 'I'm going too. So is Trevor.'

Back in class, Trevor was slicking back his dark hair, using Susan as a shield so that teacher wouldn't see him. 'You're going to give it a try? Good!' Putting away his comb, he leaned behind Niall to give me a pat on the head. The spot where his hand touched burned for ages.

It was mad over the next few days. Every time teacher was out of the room we talked about cross-country ditches, wide rivers and solid fences, the number of miles our ponies would have to gallop and the time allowed to do the course. And our chances of getting a place on the team. There were only four places and already it looked as if the whole school was competing.

Babs never joined the discussions. She and Katie were together most of the time. I didn't see much of her. What with the extra homework, more gym, Paula and the ponies, I never seemed to have a minute.

At first I wasn't too happy when Dick offered us a patch of land he owned as grazing for Bluebell. Not until Dad explained that our paddock was getting 'horse sick' and Bluebell needed good pasture as well as pony nuts for extra stamina.

I wanted her near me. We had made very good progress with her training and schooling; also the Cross-Country competition was coming closer. But Dad said it would be only for a week or so.

Dick's land was near Old Miley's road, nearly a mile away, west of the village. Dick himself visited her in the morning and in the evening Dad and I gave her fresh water and brushed her down. She had plenty of grass but I was uneasy. Dick's field, at the end of a laneway, was hidden from view of the road behind Raymond Buckley's house. She had no company and she whinnied anxiously when we left her.

'Paula and Babs are my best friends. I just can't make up my mind which one is my *very* best friend.' It was just before bedtime. I was curled up in the couch in front of the warm range, drinking cocoa and chatting with Mam, when

Dad loomed out of the darkness and stood at the door in the bright light. 'Bluebell is gone missing.'

I avoided his eyes. 'Are you sure?'

'I'm sure.' Small drops gleamed on his forehead. 'I searched all around the field. I couldn't even find a break in the fence where she could have got out.' He hesitated. 'Unless, she went in among the trees, but, she would have come when I called.'

'What about the gate?' Mam said quickly. 'Could someone have left it open?'

'It was closed. And locked.'

Pulling on an old track-suit over my pyjamas, I thought, 'She's gone into the trees and he's missed her in the dark.' I was supposed to call to see her after school, but there was no time, with gym and all. I'd forgotten that Dick would be away at his cousin's funeral.

We walked the field. It was a black night, watered down by a small foggy moon. I hummed to myself, eyes peering through the small windows of light opened by our torches in front of us. Now and then we stopped and sang out her name, straining to hear her soft whinny, but all we got back in reply was the faint echo of our voices and the uneasy rustling of the shadowy trees. I was confident she was close by. Yet everything seemed very far off. Getting from one end of the field to the other, a short distance in daylight, seemed to take for ever; we were like insects creeping about an enormous, empty, dark bowl.

Searching through the trees and bushes, I kept close to Dad. Twice we approached what we thought was her bulky outline, and waited for movement but none came. Mam's voice sounded shaky in the dark, 'I'm going home to make some phone calls. One of the neighbours is bound to have seen her.' Buckley's house in front of us was in darkness.

Dad was shining his torch along by the ditches looking for marks in the soft earth. We crossed the ditch into the next field. 'She could have gone over that bank there.'

Once I thought I heard a neigh on my left and strained for the sight of two small ears standing against the moon, the solid outline of her shape. But when we got there, I was no longer confident it was she, or if it were, that she was anywhere near by.

New lights were approaching, crossing over the ditch towards us.

'Hi.' Paula's face was pale in the gloom. Niall, beside her, shaking himself, sounded like Bluebell freeing herself of the dust of the day. I was confident again.

'I called Trevor but he's off to the disco.' He sounded anxious. 'Is your pony stolen or what?'

'No. She just strayed. She's around here somewhere.' Their well-wrapped figures briefly blocked out the chill night air.

Mam was in a group with other figures, speaking in a low voice to Dad. 'I phoned the neighbours. And there is no reply from Buckley's. They must be away.'

I asked, 'Did you try Tippings?'

'Yes, Babs said they had seen nothing either.'

Niall's head jerked upright as if he had suddenly become awake. 'Hey! I saw Babs and her kid brother in Buckley's yard. That was before teatime.'

I said thoughtfully, 'Jack might know something. Will we call up there now?'

'Might as well give it a go.' Paula stepped out on to the road. Niall and I followed. Our feet skated across the dim tarred surface as we hurried along, not saying much.

Babs opened the door just wide enough to stick her head out, a thin shaft of light coming through from the hallway behind her. 'Hi.' The smile was around her mouth only. 'You're looking for Bluebell? She's in Dick's field as far as I know.'

'She's missing.'

'Sorryeee. I wouldn't know about that.' The light on the doorstep grew narrower.

But Niall took a step forward and said, 'You were down there this evening.'

'I wasn't.'

'But I saw you!'

Suddenly a fuzzy head pushed out past her. It was her little brother Jack. 'Me and Babs saw your pony,' he said. 'She was tearin' around Buckley's lawn, kickin' and fartin' and firin' up dirt at the windows. Babs chased him out on to the road.'

The smile left Babs' face. Viciously she elbowed him back. 'Go to bed!'

All at once it felt very cold on the doorstep. Slowly I said, 'Babs, did you chase Bluebell out on to the road?'

Like a snake getting ready to strike her head darted back, green eyes narrowing to slits. 'If you'd like to know, she broke into Buckley's yard and was eating Mrs Buckley's washing off the line. We had to let her out. She was dangerous.'

Jack stuck his head out again. 'Babs was tryin' to catch her to give me and Ray a ride. We had a lasso and everything. Babs nearly got it on to her ear. Didn't you, Babs?'

'I didn't!' Babs' elbow swung again and he disappeared with a yelp. She glared at us. 'Anyway, ponies can't go around rooting up other people's lawns and making a nuisance of themselves. Only crazy ponies do that.'

'But why did you chase her out on to the road?' My voice sounded puzzled. The awfulness of what she had done was only slowly sinking in.

'I didn't chase her,' she said in a high-pitched voice. 'She just got out. It was an accident.'

I asked numbly, 'Which way did she run?'

'Don't ask me.'

'Celbridge.' A muffled reply came from behind. 'Me and Ray saw her.'

Babs' short laugh broke into bits about the small lighted patch, as we stood there in silence looking at her. 'Anyway, why make such a big deal about it!'

Paula took a few steps towards her. 'You mean,' she said in hushed tones, 'you knew she was out of the public road, where she could get killed. And you told no one.'

'You're thick, Babs,' said Niall. 'Ya know that,'

'Oh shuddup.' Babs glared at him.

Niall leaned forward threateningly but I cut in between them. 'What time was it?' Bluebell had to be found before she strayed too far.

Babs looked stubborn, as if she wasn't going to answer, then muttered, 'Six o'clock.'

It was now more than four hours later. Bluebell was used to completing a five-mile hack in one hour. She could be a long way from here.

'Let's go,' I turned away from the door.

'We'll get ya again for this. Don't you worry.' Niall was still in an angry mood.

'Oh yeah?' Babs was still defiant.

'C'mon,' I said again. 'We're wasting time.' The three of us hurried away down the dim path.

Her sudden scream stopped us in our tracks. 'I hope you never find your pony, Sarah.'

'C'mon,' Paula urged.

Her scream rang out again. 'And that she's now lyin' squashed on the road after gettin' knocked down by a juggernaut. And that her head is sliced off and that you have to put her in a bag to bury her!'

There was the sound of a door banging shut, and her words echoed hollowly in the darkening world around us. Paula pushed me forward. 'How could she! Sarah, I don't understand how you could ever have been best friends with her!'

Niall added, 'She's trouble. I mean, with friends like that, who needs enemies?'

I said nothing, still shocked at what Babs had said. Now and then the torch went on a quivering search through the parting blackness. I thought of my frightened pony wandering the wide world, alone for the first time, or lying mashed and bleeding under the wheels of a truck.

We went back to where the silent group had gathered in the roadway, eyes and ears pitched for a sight or sound of her beyond the torchlights.

Mr Dealy said that she was not on the main road. He would have seen her as he had driven over that way.

Dad added, 'If those youngsters scared her and drove her off, she won't come back. We'll have to go after her. It's not as if she simply took fright.'

Mam was still prepared to defend Babs. 'I'm sure it was all a mistake. She would not have let her out deliberately.'

'Mam, it was no mistake.' I tried to keep my voice light. 'If she let Bluebell out accidentally, why didn't she tell us immediately? If Niall hadn't seen her in Buckley's yard, we'd never have known what had happened to Bluebell.'

Mam snapped off her light. 'We can do nothing more until morning. Let's go home and get some sleep. We have a long search ahead of us tomorrow.'

Paula was allowed to stay over at our house but we didn't really sleep. Still, in the morning I didn't feel tired.

Dad was in the kitchen. His head bowed and his long legs were scattered. Out through the window the paddock looked bleak and bare under the grey sky.

Mam was bustling about as if nothing had happened. 'You're up early, girls.' She looked at us vaguely. 'Would you like a fry?' She went for the pan and came back with a saucer. Then she hurried to the study to check if the 'phone was ringing. Paula quietly fetched the pan from the press beside the cooker and I showed her the rashers and sausages.

'Thanks, Paula,' Mam breezed back in. 'I'll go ahead and make some 'phone calls.'

A knock sounded on the door. It was Niall, carrying a knapsack and looking wide-awake. 'Don't worry, Sarah.

I'm great for finding things. And I have my Granny's Saint Jude with me.' He pulled a medal from the pocket of his anorak and showed it to us.

The saint of hopeless cases! But there was going to be nothing hopeless about this search. Pushing back my plate, I said to Dad, 'We'd better get going. She's probably grazing in some field waiting for us.'

All of a sudden Dad seemed old, his forehead scrunched up with wrinkles. He said heavily, 'I checked the Lucan and Celbridge roads this morning – and on to Maynooth and nobody had seen a sight of a pony . . .' He stopped. Looked over at Mam.

That figured. Bluebell was chased and badly frightened and she wanted to get well away from the scene of fright.

Then Mam said, 'Dad is afraid that maybe Bluebell was stolen.'

There was a short silence. Paula was the first to speak, her eyes dark with concern. 'Who'd take her?'

'Don't worry.' I suddenly realised that Dad had his arms around me and that my heart was pounding like a gianormous swatch watch. 'Maybe some youngsters out for a joyride.'

Galloping, galloping her through the night. Deserting her on the roadway where she had collapsed, in a burnt-out heap, in front of a speeding lorry. Her head in a bag, red and bleeding.

His shoulder was strong and encouraging. 'Don't worry. We'll find her.' He smiled at me. 'After all, there aren't many ponies like her.'

He turned to Mam. 'Ann, did you ring the Garda Station?'

Mam came over, smiling brightly. 'Yes. I got through eventually. They want you to call there immediately to enter a full description. Then they'll send it to all Garda Stations.'

I got up, signalling to Paula who had almost finished her

fry. Niall was stuffing the last remaining sausage into his mouth as he carried the plates to the sink.

Dad had got to his feet too. 'We'd better get on the move.'

The garda handed me a diagram of a horse and helped me to fill it in. White markings had to be shown in red. 'Other Body Markings?' I wrote down that she had a wall eye.

'What about whorls?' He had crinkly brown eyes like Bono.

'She has a blaze,' I answered. 'Right in the middle of her forehead.'

'Like the words of the song. Anywhere else?' he paused with his pen to explain. 'A whorl, like a fingerprint, can make for positive identification.'

I told him she had a whorl each side mid-crest, one above each stifle.

'Any other markings? Scars? No? That's fine.'

He called to another garda. 'Willie, will you get out this description?'

'Not exactly Shergar, is he?' The other garda grinned and went off.

'Who's Shergar,' whispered Paula.

'A famous racehorse,' Niall mumbled.

Dad's step was heavy behind us. 'I'd like to see the Superintendent, if I may.' He was directed down a corridor.

From the distance I heard a voice I didn't recognise. Someone was saying, 'It's entered on our list . . . looking for a needle in a haystack . . .'

My father's voice came through clearly, 'I get the message. The larceny of this pony is not on the list of your priorities.'

'Mr Quinn, in this region alone we've had seven crimes of murder so far this year. There were twelve last year . . . Now, what did you say the value of the pony was?'

The garda leaned over the counter. 'Look,' his brown

eyes were gentle, 'I know what it's like for you, Sarah. But don't worry, we'll find your pony all right.'

I nodded. 'Where do you think she might be?'

He shrugged. 'Probably grazing happily on some green or in someone's garden. Pity you didn't have her micro-chipped for identification.'

'What's that?' Niall asked.

'It's done with all valuable animals now. The vet inserts a tiny computer chip under the horse's skin and the animal can easily be identified as the number is picked up by an electronic scanner. And then there's freeze marking.'

'Hey, man, that sounds cool,' said Niall 'I think I'll get my dad on to that.

Paula said, 'You'd better find out what it costs first.'

Dad strode up. 'Right, we'll go.'

'If we get any lead we'll get in touch right away.' The garda opened the door. 'By the way, Sarah, watch out for the "Crimeline" programme on RTE. It could be of interest.'

'Thanks, garda.'

At home, Mam was making sandwiches. 'The neighbours will be here before eleven to plan the search.'

'Listen, Mam, we're doing the search by the canal.

Bono jumped up to the sound of car doors slamming. Trevor and his dad had arrived.

The morning was bright and calm as we climbed out of Mam's car at the Grand Canal bridge at Hazelhatch and set off towards Dublin.

'What makes you think your pony went this way?' began Trevor. He took from his knapsack a large folded map, an engineer's compass and something marked Survival Kit.

'It's just a feeling she has, right?'

'A feeling? Oh, great!'

Paula said laughingly, 'I think there's a bit of a bushman in you, Trevor.'

'Gawd almighty, Trevor,' Niall shouted to him, 'You'd think we were going to survey the Amazon. We're checking out the Grand Canal towards Clondalkin.'

Paula trotted after Niall down the tow-path. 'Let's go walkalong,' she sang out.

But Trevor was still frowning at the map.

'Look,' I stayed back with him and helped him to fold it, 'it's not just a feeling. Bluebell was lonely when she broke into Buckley's – she had plenty of grass. She would have seen the cattle down there and headed this way.'

'Cattle?' Trevor put away his compass.

'She likes cattle.'

We followed Paula and Niall along by the slate-coloured water. Where a curious bullock had his head over the fence, we noted a small heap of horse dung. Niall on his haunches examined them. 'I reckon that's Bluebell's,' he announced.

She must have gone on. Under the shade of a sally-tree where water had ponded I found some small hoofmarks.

Niall climbed the tree but could see nothing. Trevor was perspiring and he unloaded some of his gear on to Niall who, like Paula and I, had only a light knapsack.

'Look!' Paula carefully held up a strand of barbed-wire to show small bunches of hair that were stuck to the barbs. Dark grey. Unmistakably Bluebell's. Heart thumping, I mooched in the grass looking for a tell-tale trail of red.

'Brilliant bit of detective work, Paula,' drawled Trevor. 'Nice one,' agreed Niall. We hurried on.

I felt that any second now Bluebell's whinny would come echoing over the still water.

On the huge timber boom of the canal-lock gate near the old mill we rested and ate our snacks. My eyes scanned the flat farmland and the public road and I thought of Grandad. He comes rolling along in his old jeep. We all hop in and ride up the hill home and there is Bluebell looking at us from her paddock, giving one almighty whinny of surprise and welcome.

'Would that pub serve us some crisps?' Niall, beside me, had his eyes fixed on the sign, 'Collander's 12th Lock Bar and Lounge', his tongue working the silver-foil wrapping like a pony at a salt lick.

'That pub serves nothing. It's a burnt-out ruin.' Paula punched him and jumped to her feet. 'C'mon mate! You won't die for a few hours.'

Further up we found more faded hoofmarks. A man and woman waved from a passing barge and I called out, 'Did you see a small grey pony with a white face?'

The man pointed downstream and shouted, 'This morning, early.'

Our steps quickened again. Another train roared past on our left. Under an overcast sky, the Round Tower of Clondalkin came into view. Still no sign of her.

Trevor, hot and sweaty, flung his gear on the ground. 'Look, you guys, I'm not sure about this search, this canal goes on for ever. We could never keep up with a horse. If we get to Clondalkin, I'll give my old man a tinkle to pick us up. I've dosh for chips.'

Niall was resting on one leg, kicking with the other, like a pony bothered by flies. 'You know,' he said, 'I reckon thieves could get a pony north of the Border in a few hours.'

Paula's jaw stuck out sharply. 'I vote we keep searching.'

Pointing to the horses grazing on the other side of the canal, I told them this could have enticed Bluebell on and I was right. There were the skid marks and hoof prints.

The terrain changed. Through the bushes we could see the grey and brown roofs of houses and factory buildings. The sky overhead was like a pan of boiling water.

Trevor was limping. 'Oh great,' he said in disgust, showing us the soft blister on his big toe.

We left him at the Lock and Key pub to ring his dad's mobile and meet us later. An old man digging the garden told us that some young boys chased a pony down the canal bank this morning. 'A dark grey, but she was too smart for them.' It was Bluebell for sure. As Grandad said the day she arrived, 'A very smart pony.'

The ground by the canal was tattoed with debris, scrap cars, caravans and heaps of rubble. We climbed over knocked-down fences and dusty thorn bushes to check out a herd of shaggy horses and ponies. No need for a closer look. Bluebell with her fine grey colouring would be easily distinguished.

'I wonder is this EC set-aside land,' said Paula. Her hand was bleeding from the scrapes.

Niall turned. He was holding the sleeve of his new denim jacket where it had torn. 'C'mon you guys . . .' but what he said was drowned in the roar of a big heavy juggernaut on the motorway above our heads. After that, all other sounds seemed to fade.

From faraway Paula was asking if I really thought Bluebell had come this far.

My mouth opened but no words came. I felt our search was doomed. I'd lost my pony. Up until now I could sniff Bluebell off the clear canal water, sense the light marks of her hooves in the mud under my feet, taste the flecks of green froth on the light breeze, hear her soft whinny on the overhead wires. Now, the angry rumble of a juggernaut had swept out everything. Everything only this awful dead feeling.

'I think Bluebell was here.' Niall was staring at me. 'Sarah, didn't Buster Harty's horse walk from Celbridge to Galway in two days? So why couldn't Bluebell make it this far?'

Paula nodded and I was hopeful again.

'Are you looking for a small grey horse?' A boy flicked his rod in the water.

'Sure thing, man,' said Niall.

The boy said, 'I saw a white-faced grey this morning in a strange place. In Brooks Thomas' yard in Bluebell.'

'Did he say Bluebell?' I asked. But the others were busily waving at some figures on the humpbacked bridge.

It was Mam and Dad and Mr Boylan.

In the jeep, Dad turned to us in the back. 'Yes, the gardai in Ballyfermot here got that same report but the security man at Brooks' knew nothing about it. 'Anyway,' he added, 'there's no guarantee it was Bluebell.'

'There are more horses around here than on the Curragh,' said Mr Boylan.

Mam, sitting between him and Dad, cleared her throat sharply. 'We mustn't forget "Crimeline",' she said.

Dad opened the gate and we drove in. The paddock looked bleak and wasted, empty apart from a lone magpie chattering to himself in the dusk.

The report on Bluebell's disappearance came on television straight after the story of a business fraud in Dublin.

'The next item concerns the larceny of a pony,' said the bean-garda. 'Horse owners and children should keep an eye out for a dark grey pony with a white blaze and four white socks. It was probably stolen last Friday, from a field beside the riding-school at Griffeen, County Dublin. It may be offered for sale privately or through equestrian centres. If you have any news of its whereabouts, telephone 01-850405060.'

We switched off. There was silence. Then Mam said brightly. 'Now, I think we'll find her. The whole country will be out looking for her.'

I felt tired and hungry, but I couldn't eat or sleep. In my room the strange dead feeling would sweep through me, staying longer each time. My head began to throb.

'Are you all right?' Sarah's mother was anxiously bending over her.

'Mam, I can't sleep.' There was terror in Sarah's voice, as if she had woken from a terrible nightmare. 'I'm afraid the fairies will take me.'

A hand on her damp forehead. 'Go to sleep,' she whispered. 'There is nothing to be afraid of. You've just had a bad dream.'

She was back in a short time with Sarah's father.

'Dad! Listen!' Sarah was sitting up in her bed, lips trembling, eyes widened, hands stretched out in front of her. 'They're calling me. I can hear the horses' hooves.'

She tried to get out of bed, but her father was by her side, gently but firmly restraining her. 'There's no hurry,' he soothed, placing her down on the pillows again. 'The fairies can wait until morning. I'll tell them. You can just sleep on until I call you.' Nodding to his wife, he left the room to make a 'phone call.

Her mother sat by Sarah's bed, holding her hot, sweaty hand.

'Listen! I can hear them again.' Sarah's grip tightened, looking at her mother with glazed eyes and fear, unable to decide if she was a witch or a living being.

'That's only your own pony, Bluebell,' her mother's voice was a sigh more than a whisper. 'Say your prayers. You have a guardian anger. He'll protect you.'

Sarah was sitting up in bed again, her eyes wide open, gazing in terror at the gleam of light penetrating through the curtains. 'I can hear the wild horses. Mam, can you hear them?' Cocking her head, breathing quickly.

She was silent for a moment as her mother desperately searched her brain for a remedy, an antidote. 'Sarah. If the fairies can't go inside a circular line, how come they can go into their fort? That's round, it's circular.'

That seemed to work and she lay down on the pillow.

Her mother whispered, 'Say your prayers now.'

'No! I have this!' Sarah put her hand under her pillow and pulled out a small silver horseshoe that gleamed dimly in the light. With her eyes on the shoe, she smiled palely. 'That's for good luck.'

When her mother tried to ease it from her grasp, she snatched it away. Hiding it under her pillow again, her eyes flickered for a moment. 'The horses,' she mumbled. 'They're pookahs. I keep thinking of them.'

A troubled look crossed her mother's face. 'Those things don't exist any more. They've all gone away. St Patrick banished them.' Repeating it until Sarah's eyes shut and her body relaxed a little, she managed to steal from the room.

'Mam,' Sarah was awake again. Getting no reply, she slowly climbed out of bed and walked to the window. Where was that whinny coming from? She had to know. Slowly she pulled back the curtain, heart thumping all the time, afraid of what she might see and ready to scream and shut her eyes. Outside in the moonlight, ghostly clouds were sailing in the bright sky. A white face peered out at her from the shadows. Beside it was the small still outline of a dog.

Greatly comforted, she got back into bed and said her prayers.

My brain must have almost shut down for a while and my

memory is cloudy like a dream. Dad said I slept for 'about a week'.

He was in the kitchen when I ran in. 'You're up. And you look so tall!'

'Bluebell! I've grown too big for her!'

'Sarah!'

I ran out of the house and down to the paddock, legs and whole body feeling heavy.

'She's gone. Where is she?' Breathless, heart pounding. I ran down the driveway, in under the fence and down to the oak-tree. I thought I glimpsed a white shaggy face. But no.

'Dad, do you think we'll ever get her back?'

'We haven't traced her yet but I know we will. The whole country is looking for her.'

The gate creaked open. It was Paula, and with her were Niall and Trevor.

Niall kicked at a thistle. 'Trevor has something to tell you.' He was so excited his voice was stuttery.

Trevor began, 'Some guy rang our stables yesterday, he said he had a message about the missing pony on "Crimeline". I didn't give him your telephone number. He sounded a bit dodgy to me. He said to give you a message – I wrote it down.' He pulled out a slip of paper.

'You read it,' I said, pushing it back to him with a shaky hand.

He read out, 'Smithfield market, Tully's corner, this Sunday, eleven o'clock.' Trevor stopped. 'He said to tell no one and the "shades" were not to hear about it. I'm not even sure I should have told you.'

Niall interrupted, 'Maybe we should go to the "shades", I mean the cops.'

'I wouldn't bother,' Trevor drawled. 'It's probably a bum steer.'

Paula said quietly, 'It's worth a try, anyhow.'

Later, from my bed, I could hear Mam and Dad talking.

Mam said, 'Sarah wants to go to Smithfield tomorrow.

And Dick has promised to take her when he goes to Mass.'

Dad's voice was low. 'Ann, it's extremely unlikely that Bluebell will be there. That area is too well policed nowadays, with DSPCA officers and gardai. The thieves wouldn't risk it. Still, if she wants to go . . .'

I sat up and read the note again.

Dick's dog Robbie sat in the back seat between Niall and Paula, while Bono lay at my feet, where he had landed after scrambling in.

'Where's Trevor?'

Niall gave a loud snort, like a pony sneezing. 'He's going to the races at Leopardstown with his dad. He'll ring later.'

We arrived early at Smithfield. With a pinch of window open and door unlocked, Dick gave Robbie charge of his car. 'I'll see you here at one o'clock.' I had quite a while to wait. A few horses and ponies were being ridden about carelessly. Pony-Club riding rules did not apply in these parts. We walked the cobblestones between the knots of people and horses, alert to any newcomers.

The crowd grew almost imperceptibly. Paula nudged me to look at a small Shetland pony paraded by a man holding the end of a much knotted blue nylon rope. She whispered furiously, 'Look. That's disgraceful! How can that poor animal even walk with those turned up feet!' She went off in search of a DSPCA officer.

I checked my watch again. On the footpath strange hens and turkeys were being unloaded from a van. 'Look, bantam cocks, for fighting,' Niall went over for a closer look.

'Are you buyin', little girl?' a man with enormous white side whiskers that curled outwards from his red face was standing beside me.

'No, thanks.' I suddenly realised that I'd been staring at his pony. It was bay coloured with a dish face and a hollow back. It didn't look at all like Bluebell but something in the face reminded me of her. A pony in need of care.

We went back to Tullys and waited but no one came. This place was deserted.

We walked back to the cafe. Nearby an argument was going on between a man in a hat and a boy on a chestnut horse. The horse was fine-boned like a thoroughbred, in good condition, although it was sweating nervously.

The boy was shaking his head. 'No, sir. I can't trot her on the cobblestones. This ground is too rough and uneven.'

'I know that boy,' Paula murmured in my ear. 'He was at Irish College.'

Niall looked at her in surprise. 'I didn't know you had to learn Irish.'

'I didn't have to. I just wanted to . . . Let's go over and talk to him.'

Muttered Niall, 'He looks like a traveller. Are you sure he was at Irish College?'

'I'm sure. He was on a scholarship,' Paula said. There was a note of excitement in her voice. 'A quiet bloke, didn't bother with any of us much. I didn't know he was into horses. Come on over.'

Niall wasn't too keen. But already Paula was on her way, pulling me with her. The man had moved away.

The boy, who sat erect in the saddle, was about my own age and size, wearing a stained green anorak and runners. He was stroking the mare but she still looked agitated and was throwing her head about.

'Do you remember me?' Paula smiled up at him.

'Yeah.' His hand moved up and down, petting the mare gently. Two big golden rings glinted on his fingers.

Paula persevered. 'Irish College was great crack, wasn't it?' she asked conversationally.

He nodded, black eyes flickering. He wasn't too friendly.

'Is she yours?' Niall dug his hands into his pockets and nodded at the mare.

'No, I'm just riding her for a fella.' The boy's voice was low and his lips barely moved. 'I take care of her. I ride her

and look after her.'

I saw that the hooves were well trimmed, the mane and tail perfectly groomed.

For some reason I drew closer, and patted the mare's steaming neck. 'She's the nicest animal here,' I said. 'What's her name?'

'Star.'

'What will you do when she's sold?' Was he, too, going to lose a faithful friend?

His hand stopped moving on the far side of his horse's neck. The black eyes looked sharply at me, as sharp as ice on the deep dark canal. Then the hand moved again. 'I have a new one. Got a present from my dead mother.'

His mare had become more relaxed, chomping on the bit. I took my hand away and looked over towards Tully's store. Only a few stragglers were being led about. I could see no pony resembling Bluebell. Dad and Mr Boylan had been right. Bluebell was not coming.

The mare was tossing her head again and I went to soothe her fine neck. She cleaned her white foaming mouth on my coat. 'What does your new pony look like?'

'She's a topper!' The boy suddenly came alive, his hand moving swiftly, jerking in excitement. 'Like a streak of silver. Fast. And she has four new shoes. My mare never had shoes. And her legs are fine and clean, built for speed. I could ride to Galway on her.'

'What's her name?'

'She has no name yet. I can pick any name I like. But she's some prancer.'

'Dancer?' Like Bluebell. As the cobblestones bubbled up and down, threatening to capsize horses and people. I tried to keep my feet under me. 'My pony was like that but she was stolen. She was a grey, with a white mane.'

His hand hesitated on the mane. 'Her only one little fault . . . nothing much . . .'

I kept petting the horse, not able to move on the shifting cobble-stones. 'Did you say a wall-eye?'

He looked down at me and stared. The ice cracked in the black eyes. He bowed his head and spoke in a mumbled whisper. But I heard him. I heard him clearly.

With that he sat erect and wheeled his horse around and rode off, the man who was watching all along, hurrying after him.

Niall was beside me. 'What was he saying to you?' looking at me curiously. 'Is he a traveller or what?'

'Bluebell, The Blackhorse Inn. The car park. He's to meet us within the hour. Where's Dick? Where's Paula?'

'Look, Sarah, what are you talking about? Maybe we should get the guards. I don't like the look of that guy. And now he's after disappearing. You wouldn't know what he is planning. He might have a gang waiting.'

'I don't think so, Niall.'

'Blackhorse Inn?' Dick chuckled. 'That's a pub. In

Inchicore. Sure we'll drive over.'

'The guy seems okay.' said Paula. 'He probably is on the level. Anyway, I have his name and address somewhere. At Gaeltacht we all promised we'd write but of course we never did.'

Dick sat and read the Sunday newspapers in the public-house car park while we searched.

In the nearby Industrial Estate we kept our eyes and ears open as we passed by locked-up factories and warehouses. A red shed at the top of a slope attracted our attention, but it was barred up and there was no sound from inside. Close to the flats were old lanes and dilapidated buildings.

'She could be hidden here and we'd never find her, unless she kicked up a racket or gave a mighty whinny.' Niall sounded gloomy.

Dick had talked to people in the pub. He had no news. 'Don't worry, she'll turn up,' he said.

'We've just one more place to check, Dick.'

'I'll be turning.' When he opened the car door, Bono hopped out. We walked down by the side of the pub through the bollards and along the path, down by an old disused graveyard. A narrow path lay empty before us once more. The three of us looked at it in silence. There was no sign of the boy or my pony. This was the end of the search. It was time to go.

A lapping sound came to our ears from the far side of a high embankment.

'It's Bono,' said Paula. 'I'll get him.'

She scaled the embankment. At her cry we climbed up after her and found her kneeling near the doorway of a small chapel, pointing at a plastic bucket full of water. Beside it was an old biscuit tin with a few grains of oats.

'There must be a horse here,' Niall gasped.

Next thing Bono brushed against me. I looked down to see that he had a lump of horse dung in his mouth.

'Could it be Bluebell?' Paula looked at me thoughtfully.

'She was here.' I turned away, knowing that my pony was already far away. Otherwise she could have recognised my footstep, given a whinny.

'At least she had plenty of food and water,' Paula said. 'He must have fed her well last night, knowing he would be at Smithfield this morning. She is probably in good condition.'

'And if she's fit,' Niall added cheerfully, 'she'll survive anything.'

We were hurrying back to tell Dick when an old woman came out of one of the houses.

'Are ye looking for the little horse?' she asked. 'A boy came by here leading a pony not so long ago at all. These other fellows tried to snatch it away from him and there was a terrible racket. Then I seen the little horse galloping off like fork lightning.

'Which way?' we said together.

She pointed towards the main road. Towards home!

Dad met us at the door, his hair standing straight up. 'I was just about to ring the Pound in Saggart,' he said. 'The garda in Ballyfermot said that some horses had just been picked up and taken there.'

'Hello?' A man's voice answered.

'Have you got a pony up there?' My voice sounded a few octaves higher than usual.

'We have two.'

'Is one a grey filly?'

There was a short silence at the other end. Then, 'Any distinguishing marks?'

'She has a wall-eye.'

The voice said abruptly, 'You'd better come up and have a look.'

In the Pound a few skewbald horses were eating hay. The keeper was helpful. He led us to a small field where a

Shetland pony was grazing. 'Keep well away from that one,' he warned. 'She'd kill you with a kick.'

But where was the second pony? We followed him on down the field. He was pointing at a round grey heap that rose out of the grass. My knee started to hop, with an increasing rhythm. It stirred, and a head with a white blaze and two small erect ears turned to us.

'Bluebell!' Her wild whinny rang out, full of sorrow and relief.

'She's exhausted,' the Pound keeper said. 'But she's none the worst for wear, apart from a few skin cuts. And she has cast a shoe.' He added, 'You were lucky to find her in such good shape.'

She had dragged herself to her feet and I stayed supporting her, with my face buried in the soft fur of her neck for a long time.

She licked the salt off my face with delight.

After Mr Boylan's horse-box drove out through the gate, I waited at the fence to watch Bluebell grazing in the paddock. 'You know,' turning to Paula and Niall, 'only for the boy at Smithfield we might never have found her.'

'Yeah,' Paula said. 'I can give you his address if you want to contact him. I'm sure he'd like to know Bluebell is okay.'

'Thanks.'

Niall kicked at the fence. 'I dunno would it be a good idea. I mean, what's the point in getting in touch with the thief unless you want to put him in jail?'

'You don't think he stole her, do you?' I asked. 'He wouldn't! No way!'

Paula's forehead was furrowed but she said nothing.

Niall's feet shuffled. 'He could have found her wandering about.'

That night, Mam and Dad took the three of us to The Square where we shared a huge pizza with loads of garlic bread, the best I've ever tasted in my life, almost.

'Pity Trevor is missing out,' said Niall, wiping his jaws with his serviette. He wasn't back yet from Leopardstown.

Mam had mentioned inviting Babs along with us.

'Oh great, Mam,' I had said sarcastically. 'Babs was my best friend. Why did she chase my pony out on the road? I'm never going to speak to her again. It's true what Paula says. She is treacherous.'

And Niall and Paula agreed when I told them.

'It doesn't always work out like that,' Mam said later, as she bent to kiss me goodnight.

'I hate Babs.' I was already half asleep, and feeling like I hadn't slept for a whole year. 'I'll never speak to her again. I hate having to see her in school.'

'Sarah,' Mam said softly, 'not everyone is as lucky as you, with a pony, a Mam and Dad who are mad about you, good friends. Life is not as easy for other girls and boys. For some, school can be a haven from home.'

A haven? What was she talking about! Tired as I was, Mam had to be put right on that one. I sat up. 'You think she's poor? She's not, Mam. She's rich. Her dad gave me a fiver at the pub when I was out with Grandad. She's not poor. And what about all the perfume she gets. And the Arab horse. And her dad is getting a private plane.'

'Just think about what I said, will you? Good night.'

My eyes closed again. 'Everyone is not as lucky as you are,' What was she on about? My pony could have been killed.

The tired look gradually cleared from Bluebell's face, and her whinny grew soft again like the fur on her neck. Coming in from school, I had long chats with her over the hedge and she was madly interested in my school report.

Which was good, by the way!

14 CROSS COUNTRY

Nearly everyone had heard about Bluebell on the telly. Even Babs – Katie told me.

'I'll get even with her. So I will.' Niall is rooting for his history copy under the desk, pulling it out, dog-eared, slaps it open. He threw another look over at Babs standing in the corner. This was her third day without doing her homework and teacher was deciding what to do with her.

At Assembly, the headmistress announced that those who wanted to be chosen for the school team in the Pony Inter-Schools Challenge Cross-Country and Show Jumping would first have to enter the qualifying competition in Kill.

'Give your names to the secretary, Miss Daly, within the week.'

I really wanted to make that team and represent our school. I was hoping the three of us would qualify – and Trevor too. At the last minute Niall had persuaded him to put his name down.

Coming home on the bus, Katie sat beside me. Babs had a big puss on her and sat staring out of the window. Why should *she* be feeling hurt? I was the one who was betrayed. It was my pony that was stolen. But no. Babs was behaving as if I were the one who had done wrong. That I was the one who should apologise.

Next day at playtime, I said to Paula, 'Maybe we should ask Babs to walk around with us.'

'No, leave her there.' Paula's lips tightened.

But what Mam had said haunted me. Was I being unfair?

I made up my mind to call up to her after school. I'd just knock at the door and say 'Hello' and come home again.

She opened the door and looked at me, eyes hostile. 'What do you want?'

'I thought I'd drop by and . . .' Then real casually, 'Can I come in?' Babs had never invited me inside her house.

She stepped back. 'My mam isn't in. I'm not allowed bring in anyone when she's not home.' She went to close the door.

Then her mother's shrill voice came from inside. 'Babs, is that your friend? Bring her in!' Babs was such a liar.

I slipped past her at the door. The hallway was dark and full of old black heavy furniture. In the lounge, her mother was sitting on a big couch with a glass in her hand and when she saw me she smiled and waved me to a chair beside her, at the same time telling Babs, 'Put on the dinner, will you, dear? And when you've done that, run upstairs and check on the baby.'

'Yes, Mother,' Babs hurried off.

'Well, Sarah, how are you?' Mrs. Tipping drained her glass, then filled it up again from the bottle on the floor beside her. 'I'm glad you called,' she said. 'We don't have many visitors. My husband travels quite a bit and leaves me on my own.'

What was she talking about? Hadn't she got a family?

She went on, 'Dennis is in New York at the moment. It's only for a few days. Dinner at Maxims, shows on Broadway.'

'Yeah, I know,' I said wistfully. 'I wish my Dad was getting a private plane.'

'Private plane?' She turned her head and stared at me for a moment. Then she started to laugh. When she finally stopped she said in a solemn voice, 'If he does, make sure you get a trip in it.' She laughed again. It was getting a bit boring with all this laughing. I wondered where Babs was and was about to get up and go when she appeared at the door with the baby in her arms.

Suddenly Mrs Tipping stiffened at the sound of a car on

the gravel outside. 'Your father is home! He wasn't due until Saturday. Quickly, Babs. Go down and put on the heat. You know how he hates it when the house is cold. And he won't have had any dinner. Take a look in the fridge. Have we any steak? No? Nothing only mince. That won't do. What about that piece of salmon? All gone? Have we any wine?' I picked up the dirty nappy off the couch beside me and helped her to sweep some glossy magazines off the table. Then she disappeared, probably to change from her dressing-gown.

Mr Tipping dumped his briefcase on the floor. Bottles clinked in the duty-free carrier bag. 'What's for dinner?'

'Just mince.'

'Mince! I should have stopped off in town and had a decent meal.' He went to the drinks cabinet.

Then he noticed me. 'Why, hello, Sarah, isn't it? Nice to see you. And how's your mother? A smart woman who keeps in touch. Always interesting to talk to. What's she doing with herself at the moment?'

'Well, she was doing a computer course,' I said. My mother a smart woman? No one had ever said that before. 'She's finished that,' I hurried on in case he lost interest. 'Now she's doing a course on automobile mechanics. She wears overalls and all.'

'Terrific!' He took a drink from his glass. Mrs Tipping had reappeared. She was wearing white make-up and looked like a vampire because her lipstick was all smudged from being put on in a hurry.

'Ah, there you are, darling. And what have you being doing with yourself since I left?"

'Nothing much.'

'Sarah here has been telling me all about her mother. Why don't you take some courses? Give you something to talk about when we go to functions. Don't forget that cock-tail party next week.'

'I'd prefer not to go. I'm not very interested in talking to those people.'

The baby began to cry. He jumped. 'God almighty. I've had a hard day. Can't someone take that child away? And what about something to eat?'

Walking back home through the fields, I thought about Babs. It was true what Mam had said. You never do know about people. Still, even if Babs had a hard time at home, why did she have to take it out on people like me? I couldn't forgive her for the awful things she had said when Bluebell was missing. No, I wasn't going to forgive her. At least not yet.

15 THE TRIALS

At Kill the qualifying competition had started. We had walked the cross-country course, splashed through the rivers and tested the solid fences that our ponies would have to jump.

'Complete the course in three minutes and twenty-five seconds,' said Miss Daly.

Paula went first. Our eyes followed her multi-coloured jersey as far as possible into the distance. We waited anxiously. She burst through the hedge and came thundering down to the finishing post.

'How did he go at the water?' I asked her.

'Fine,' nostrils flaring, breathing fast. 'Watch out for the tiger trap. The ground is now very soft.'

'What's a tiger trap?'

'You'll see it when you come to it?'

Next it was Niall on Teabag. He was checking the stopwatch Trevor had loaned him as he rode into the flagged finish splattered in mud.

We had a slow start off. But Bluebell cleared the ditch and then we cantered towards the first jump, a fallen log.

Bluebell was cautious, inclined to be spooky, ready to stop if she got the least excuse, and it was difficult holding her attention as she was viewing the spectators. Then the bank, the river, and, next, the treacherous tiger trap. No bother. Bluebell was beginning to enjoy herself.

Turning towards home there was the ditch before the river. It loomed up ahead of us. And as we soared across it, I immediately looked to my left for our next obstacle, the water jump. My pony slowed and steadied her canter. We popped over the low pole and broke the clear waters with a splash. A great feeling of confidence washed over me as we surged through the river, my eyes fixed on the stone and earth bank in front. Has she the energy and power? Yes!

That evening, I placed my jacket on the grass and sat beside Bluebell who lay down near the oak tree. I gently stroked her eyelids with the palm of my hand as I had seen Dick doing. When she pushed her chin on to my knees, I softly whispered in her ear, 'You are amazing. Your first cross-country – and we're on the team to represent my school in the Inter-Schools Challenge. You know, I think this is what you and I were destined for!'

Placing my cheek against her bony one I closed my eyes and could feel her heart stirring softly. Also the vibrations of a tail smacking the ground.